EVERY SUNRISE

HOME TO HEATHER CREEK™

EVERY SUNRISE

Tricia Goyer

Guideposts
NEW YORK, NEW YORK

To Lesley, my sweet sister, who found me and ushered me into the family I didn't know but now can't imagine living without.

Acknowledgments

I'm thankful for my family . . . it's amazing how many real-life experiences make fiction exciting! John, Cory, Leslie, Nathan, Grandma, and Andrea . . . thank you for the laughter and love within the walls we call HOME.

I'm thankful for my assistant Amy Lathrop. It's great to have a second pair of eyes when I second guess myself!

I'm thankful for writer friends, Vickie McDonough, Deb Kinnard, Jenny Carlisle, Jolene Catlett, and Dennis Bates who gave me insight about growing up in the mid-west. Good stuff!

I'm thankful for the Guideposts team—the best in the business! Special thanks go to Beth Adams and Fiona Serpa for taking my story from good to great!

—Tricia Goyer

Home to Heather Creek

Before the Dawn

Sweet September

Circle of Grace

Homespun Harvest

A Patchwork Christmas

An Abundance of Blessings

Every Sunrise

EVERY SUNRISE

Chapter One

It was cold outside. It had been the coldest February Charlotte could remember in a dozen years at least, and they were only one week in. She glanced around at the ice-crusted, shimmering world their farm had transformed into overnight and reminded herself that spring would be right around the corner. Not with tomorrow's sunrise—or the next—but before long, she'd be digging in the warm earth, planting seeds for her garden. Before she knew it, she'd be griping at the kids for trailing in mud and grass clippings on their sneakers. It was a nice thought.

But today, Charlotte's boots crunched on the ground's thin crust of snow. Her warm breath made soft puffs in the air. She tucked her hands into her pockets and hurried with her grandchildren toward the little Ford Focus.

Despite the crispness in the air, she loved the way the frozen briar patches on the edge of the fence line gleamed like the crystal candleholders she kept in her dining room hutch. The candleholders were a wedding gift she had never used and only took time to admire once a month when she took them out to dust.

Maybe I should pull them out for the next family celebration, Charlotte thought as she scurried on. But she quickly pushed that thought out of her mind as she remembered last night's impromptu football game between Sam and Christopher with a pair of clean socks. The boys had too much pent-up energy and no place to expend it.

Better to keep the candlesticks tucked away. Keep them safe.

In the distance, the cottonwood trees stretched their frozen branches into the sky. Yesterday they appeared bare and uninteresting, but somehow during the hours she'd slept they'd been clothed in a glittery shroud.

"Grandma, it's awfully cold today. Are you sure it's okay for the horses to be out?" Emily asked, hurrying past her big brother Sam to keep up with Charlotte, her eyebrows scrunched in concern.

"Yes, they're fine. Uncle Pete is mucking their stalls, and then they'll go right back inside where it's nice and warm."

Britney and Stormy pranced behind the fence next to the barn as they watched Charlotte and the kids scramble to the car. The barbed wire resembled a string of fragile glass, giving the impression that the horses' slightest touch would shatter the wire into a million little pieces.

Sort of like Sam's spirit, Charlotte thought. *Sort of like Sam.*

Just like the cold wind that had swept in from the north, a chilly attitude had settled over Sam too. He'd been doing well lately—or so she thought. Last month he'd spent a weekend with Jake and Paul, and it appeared to Charlotte that he'd connected with his friends. Then—the same day the dark clouds over the north pasture blew in—Sam's attitude changed as well. In the past few days, his words had been sharp. His face drawn. His eyes downcast.

Charlotte wasn't the only one who'd noticed. Everyone had been tiptoeing around her oldest grandson lately as if his emotions would shatter as easily as the thin icicles that hung from the front porch. Even Bob had sensed Sam's sour attitude and had been easier on him. Charlotte wished she knew what was wrong. Wished she knew what to do about it.

Charlotte opened the trunk. She gently put down the bag carrying the laptop computer from Christopher's class. Ten-year-old Christopher put in his rocket and stand, and Emily laid his large display board on top of it all.

"Careful, don't put anything on top of that computer bag," Charlotte said, scooting the display board to the side.

"Grandma, it's cardboard. It's not going to hurt anything," said Emily, with a fourteen-year-old's typical disdain.

"I know, I know. But I told Miss Rivkin that I'd deliver the computer to the school in one piece. She said they usually don't let the students bring the school computers home, and she'd only agreed because I promised to watch over it." Charlotte slammed the trunk closed.

Emily smirked. "Yeah, well, thanks for giving us a ride too—since you were going all that way for the computer." Laughter burst from Emily's lips.

Charlotte chuckled at Emily's humor as she climbed in her car, shut the car door, and started the engine. Then she glanced into her rearview mirror, catching a glimpse of her oldest grandson's set jaw and downcast eyes. She felt her own smile fade.

Common sense told her that his sour attitude was mostly due to the fact that his car was broken down—yet again. But she also noticed sadness in his eyes. Sometimes he tried to hide it, but it was hard to miss.

Maybe his car breaking down is a good thing, Charlotte thought. She actually missed the times when all three kids were together, even if it was riding in the car.

Over the past week or so, Sam had spent a lot of time alone in his room. He did his chores by himself and excused himself from family movie nights. In her opinion, his time driving to and from school by himself wasn't good either. Sam was already introspective by nature—he didn't need more alone time to think.

Their seat belts clicked in unison, and Charlotte drove down the pothole-filled driveway. The tires crunched over the patches of hard, dirty snow left from the last snowfall. She felt herself shiver despite her heavy coat and her thick gloves.

Beside her on the front seat, Christopher sniffed the air. "Grandma, did you make strawberry cupcakes for our lunch?" He opened his paper lunch bag and peeked in before she had a chance to answer. His face immediately fell.

"Sorry, Christopher, just plain, ol' boring oatmeal raisin cookies—no fancy cupcakes today."

Emily leaned over the backseat. "The smell is my new lip gloss. It smells like strawberry shortcake. Want some?" She reached out her hand, pretending she was going to put it on Christopher's lips.

"Get away!" he squealed. "Lip gloss is for girls! I don't want pink lips."

"It won't make them pink." Emily settled back in her seat. "Only shiny and pretty."

"Ugh." Christopher stuck out his tongue. "That's even worse."

"I thought you liked shiny stuff. I saw shiny things flying all over the farm last weekend."

"Those were rockets, Emily, not shiny things. And they were really cool."

Charlotte glanced into the rearview mirror, catching Emily's gaze. "Don't tease him, Emily. I know you were there and just as excited about what was going on. I heard your voice on the home video."

Emily shrugged. "I know. I was just teasing. Everyone needs a little teasing now and then, right, Sam?"

Sam grunted an answer that left Charlotte guessing whether it was a yes or a no.

"I hope my science project does okay." Christopher turned to Charlotte, his face bright with excitement. "They say the top two winners in each category get to go to the *county* science fair."

Charlotte smiled at seeing her grandson excited. She said a silent prayer that he would win something. Every event, big or small, that could plug her grandchildren into the community was a plus.

"It better be good," Emily complained, "to get me out of the house at o'dark thirty."

"Well, I needed time to set everything up. I wanted to make sure I got a good spot too, because it's a cool project."

"It *is* cool," Charlotte added. "I bet they haven't seen anything like this around here. Most of the kids do tests on the soil. Or they grow things in their parents' greenhouses. I'm not sure I've ever heard of a rocket project before." She drummed her fingers on the steering wheel, trying to get them to warm up. "Christopher, when will you know if you're going on to the county science fair?"

"Next Friday, February fourteenth."

"Valentine's Day? That's an odd day. I mean with everything else going on." Charlotte's voice trailed off as she remembered how meaningful that day was when she was in high school—or how traumatic it could be.

"Do the cheerleaders still run their flower fundraiser?" Charlotte asked.

The words were barely out of her lips when Emily let out a moan. "Grandma, please don't talk about that—I've heard the stories."

"Stories?"

"Yeah, of people getting made fun of because they don't even get one flower. I heard once there was a girl who didn't come to school ever again after going home without a flower. In fact, no one has seen her since then."

"Grandma, is that true?" Christopher craned his neck to look at his sister.

"Of course not, I'm sure there are disappointed kids, but many things in life will bring that. It doesn't mean you just drop out of life."

"Personally, I think they should find another way to make money." Emily's voice took on an authoritative tone. "The only ones who like it are the popular kids, since they're guaranteed a ton of flowers. In fact, you can tell the pecking order by the number of flowers each person receives."

Christopher wrinkled up his nose. "Pecking order? Grandma, what does that mean?"

"It means that some people have it good, and then there are the rest of us—who just keep getting pecked lower and lower, with no way to escape." Sam's voice was solemn. But as soon as the words were out of his mouth he was silent again.

Charlotte looked in the rearview mirror, but Sam's hoodie was pulled over his head and he was looking out the window. If Charlotte had had any question before whether there was something brewing in Sam's head, she was certain about it now.

"Actually, it's a term that developed because of chickens," Charlotte said lightheartedly, trying to add a note of interest to the dreary conversation. "A pecking order is like a system of people who are ranked, one above the other. Just like the chickens peck at each other to display dominance, sometimes people do that too."

"Peck each other?" Christopher wrinkled his nose, and Charlotte couldn't help but laugh. Christopher rubbed his arm. "Ouch."

"Yeah, unfortunately people often like to act as if they're more important than others, despite the fact God calls us equal in his sight—"

"Which is why we should outlaw the whole fundraiser," Emily interrupted.

"Or maybe they should lock you up for being a whiner," Sam mumbled. "It's just flowers. It won't be the end of the world if you don't get one."

"What's your problem?" Emily hissed at her brother. "You've been a grump all morning. Is it because you don't have tires for that piece of junk of yours?"

"No, I got tires. Not like you cared anyway . . ."

"They're not sure what the problem is," Charlotte chimed in. "Grandpa has to take a look."

Emily seemed satisfied by this answer, but Charlotte knew it hadn't resolved anything.

They pulled up to Christopher's school, and Charlotte turned in her seat. "Emily, can you help Christopher carry his rocket into the classroom? I'll follow in a minute with the poster board."

"I don't need help, Grandma," Christopher asserted. "Everyone will think I'm a baby if Emily helps me."

"I insist. Emily, can you please help? I'll be in soon."

Charlotte's gaze met Emily's eyes, and Emily glanced at Sam as if knowing the purpose for the request.

"C'mon, Christopher. No one will think you're a baby." Emily opened the car door. "Besides I want to check out the other kids' projects—even though I know yours is going to leave them in the dust." Charlotte popped open the trunk for Emily and Christopher to retrieve the project.

Christopher carried his rocket tight to his chest. Emily put the computer bag over her shoulder and carried the stand in her hands. Charlotte said a silent prayer that Emily wouldn't drop the laptop on her way into the building.

Christopher and Emily merged with other kids heading into the double doors of the school, some of them also carrying their projects into the building.

Charlotte turned further in her seat to look at Sam.

"I can walk the rest of the way." Sam reached for the door handle.

"Not so fast."

He dropped his hand back to his lap.

"Do you want to tell me what's wrong?"

"Nothing."

They sat there for a full minute, neither saying a word. Charlotte had read once that interviewers would often use silence to encourage the people they interviewed to talk— since no one likes a void in the conversation. No one except Sam, that is.

"Fine. I'll drop it for now, but you know you can come to me with whatever problem you're having."

Sam nodded once, but kept silent.

Charlotte's mind scurried to think of something else to say, to do, to leave their parting on a more positive note. "Your birthday is coming up," she hurriedly added. "Do you have any idea what you want to do? Have a family party? Invite some friends over?"

"Hop the next plane outta here?" Sam mumbled. Then he reached for the door handle and climbed out. "Thanks for the ride, Grandma, but I better get going." He offered a small wave. As he glanced down at her through the car window, Charlotte noticed something else in Sam's gaze.

An apology.

Charlotte watched Sam amble off, then she took her keys from the ignition and looked in the still-open trunk. Christopher's display board was inside, and she couldn't help but smile as she noticed how he'd used his best handwriting on the captions under his photographs.

She carried it to the school entrance while a little boy with a large backpack struggled to open the door for her. She thought she recognized him from church—maybe he was one of the little guys from the Christmas pageant. He smiled at her, and she knew her guess was right. She remembered those missing teeth from one of the wooly sheep.

She found Christopher's classroom, the third door on the left. It was the same one Bill had had, and Pete too. Denise had been down the hall with a different teacher. Being here—with the sights of the bright posters and kids' projects on the wall, the scents of floor cleaner and Elmer's glue, the sun streaming through the tall windows—made her feel as if twenty years hadn't passed. For the briefest moment she felt a twinge of emotion, remembering her own kids at this age—so innocent, so full of laughter and mischief.

She swallowed hard as she noticed Christopher's teacher, Miss Rivkin, filing graded papers into the students' cubbies in the corner of the room. She wore a sharp navy blue suit that perfectly accented her short, red hair.

"Mrs. Stevenson, so good to see you. Christopher's setting up his project in the gym. I can show you where he is."

Charlotte knew where the gym was. She had walked these halls more times than she could count, bringing sack lunches, cupcakes on birthdays, attending basketball games. Yet she knew better than to cross "The Boss," as she often heard the kids referring to Miss Rivkin. Charlotte smiled. "Sure, lead the way. And please call me Charlotte."

Miss Rivkin's high-heeled shoes clacked on the chipped tile floor as she walked down the long hall and crossed the breezeway into the gym. Christopher had already set up his rocket and display on a long folding table. Charlotte glanced around and noticed the usual array of volcanoes, star constellations, and plants in various stages of growth.

"Thanks, Grandma." Christopher took the display board from her. "Emily told me to tell you she already headed to her school."

Christopher diligently set up his display board and checked and rechecked to make sure everything was laid out "just right." Charlotte couldn't help but smile. He seemed older than he had this morning, sitting in his Shrek pajamas at the breakfast table. More capable too.

Charlotte looked at the display board. Over the last few weeks, she'd watched the progress of the project. That included viewing the rocket's launch from her spot at the kitchen window a few days ago when Christopher, Emily, and Pete set it off in the driveway. Toby had even gotten into the act, barking and carrying on as if the rocket was a toy Christopher had picked out specifically for her. But Charlotte hadn't seen the completed display since she had gone to bed before Christopher had finished it. She was impressed. There were photographs of the different types of rockets; a hand-drawn picture of the rocket-launch liftoff, thrust phase, coast phase, and ejection; and a map printed off the Internet indicating rocket landing areas. She smiled, imagining Sam on the computer "Googling" the right information for his brother. Charlotte was sure her older grandson could find a way to order cheesecake from New York and pizza from Chicago over the Internet—and have it shipped to their house by morning.

"Mrs. Ste—I mean Charlotte—you're welcome to stay if you'd like. I assigned each of the kids a time to give their science talk, and Christopher just happens to be first this morning. He'll be meeting with the judges in less than ten minutes."

Charlotte glanced at her watch. She'd thrown a load of clothes in the dryer before she'd left. They were most likely done and wrinkling in the dryer at this very moment. Then there was the shopping she still had to do and the tractor part she was supposed to pick up for Pete at AA Tractor Supply Store. She'd already heard his speech twelve times at home.

Then again, she glanced around, realizing that through all the science projects over the years she'd never stuck around for this part. Her excuses most likely had been all the ones going through her head at this moment.

"Sure, I'd love to stay." Charlotte placed a hand on Christopher's shoulder. "If it's okay with you, that is."

His face brightened. "Yeah, cool."

"Okay." Charlotte pointed to the end of the row. "I'll wait down there so I won't be in the way."

Ten minutes later, Charlotte watched as Christopher gave his presentation.

He explained reasons he chose this project and the books he read in his research. He stated important key dates concerning rocket development, and then turned the attention of the judges toward the video he'd created with an actual rocket launch.

Christopher clicked a few buttons on the computer, and seconds later the video played. It was Pete's voice that Charlotte heard first, talking to Christopher as he shot the video.

"Okay, tell me what you're doing again?" Pete's voice asked.

On the video, Christopher knelt on the cold ground. He pulled off his gloves and laid them on the dirty snow next to his rocket, then he began fiddling with the wires at the rocket's base. "First, I'm clipping the hooks onto the igniters of the rocket. Here's one and here's the second one." He glanced at Pete videotaping only briefly, then returned to his task. "But the first one is a little bit loose so I'm going to tighten it.

"And then after I get them clipped on, I'm going to move my gloves away from the rocket base," Christopher continued. "I don't want anything flammable very close by."

"How come?" Pete's voice asked.

"Because the hot exhaust could catch something on fire.

Now, I'm attaching the igniter and the plug. The plug keeps the igniter on and when it is launched the igniter and the plug come off.

"Then I have to put the rocket on the stand. Then I have to unwind the cord."

"Uh, Christopher, do you think we should stand back?" Pete asked. Charlotte chuckled to herself as she watched the shaky camera move backward.

"Come on, Toby," Pete added.

"And now, since the hooks are clipped on, I will put the key into the hole. Press it down until the light comes on, and then it's countdown time!" Christopher grinned at the camera.

Charlotte heard Christopher, Pete, and Emily count in unison. "Five, four, three, two, one . . ."

"*Wahow!*"

"There it goes!" Emily's voice said in the video. The video followed the rocket into the air and then back down again.

"There it is," Emily called out. "It's landing on the snow!"

"Wait, Toby, no!"

Charlotte chuckled as she watched Toby pouncing on the rocket, then she trotted back to Christopher with it in her mouth, her tail wagging. The video clicked off and the team of judges burst into laughter.

"And that is my project. If you look close you can still see Toby's teeth marks, which just goes to show that rocket science is something you can really bite into. Thank you," Christopher said with a wave of his arm and a bow.

All of the judges clapped, and Charlotte clapped the hardest, much to Christopher's embarrassment and delight.

After she had given Christopher a thumbs-up and waved

good-bye, she walked to the car, remembering how just a few weeks prior Pastor Evans had given a sermon on the power of positive words. It was one of her flaws, she knew, to see all the problems rather than focusing on what was right. Fixing problems seemed to work for things like gardening, and chores, and the hundred and one things that broke down on the farm every week. Yet she could see by the look on Christopher's face that praise was necessary. Perhaps she could concentrate on offering him more praise—and Emily too.

And Sam—she still had to figure out what would help him.

Chapter Two

The scent of coffee and cinnamon rolls greeted Charlotte as she entered Mel's Place. Melody had outdone herself with her decorations this time. Large red hearts hung from the ceiling, spinning slightly with the cold breeze that had entered with Charlotte. Red tablecloths draped the tables and large heart-shaped lollipops sat in jars that were decorated to look like big gumdrops. The centerpieces reminded Charlotte of something Willy Wonka might come up with for his chocolate factory.

Melody was cleaning the display case with glass cleaner. She turned and smiled at Charlotte with cheeks as rosy as her red apron. "Charlotte Stevenson! Good to see you. You have the look in your eye."

"The look?"

"The look that says you're in need of a cup of coffee and a fresh cinnamon roll."

"Decaf please and half a roll." Charlotte patted her middle, which bulged slightly over her jeans. "It's been a long winter already, and I need to start watching what I'm putting in my mouth. It's too easy to nibble on a cookie as I'm packing the kids' lunches."

15

"You're telling me. I have the same problem." Melody walked behind the counter and pulled a clean coffee cup off the glass shelf.

"Imagine cooking pastries and snacks all day. I'll tell you, I can't wait for spring so I can do some laps around the block. In fact, that's what I told Ashley I want for my birthday—new walking shoes. She's heading to Harding with her dad next weekend to go shopping. Funny how they always do that right before my birthday."

Melody winked. "Puts them a little closer to my favorite shoe store."

Charlotte nodded. "Yes, I remember. Your birthday is right after Valentine's Day, right? Sam's birthday is just a few days before—on the eleventh."

Melody poured two cups of coffee and cut a cinnamon roll in half, setting it on two plates. Then she put the plates across from each other on the nearest table as if meeting for coffee had been the plan all along.

Melody settled into the seat with a smile. "I remember when Sam was born. It was early in the morning, and Pete mentioned it to one of his friends at school. Five minutes later news had spread around the whole town. Even though I was out of high school, at the time it seemed impossible that one of my friends could be a mom. It was only a few years later that I had Brett and then Ashley—wow, how old does that make Sam now?"

"Seventeen. Practically a man." Charlotte could hear Bob's voice in her head as she said those words: *Which means it's time to treat him like a man, Char. No letting him do kids' chores any longer. He's old enough to do the work of a man.*

Charlotte took a large bite of her roll. It was soft and

warm, and the frosting had the perfect amount of sweetness. The corners of her mouth curled into a smile as she chewed. As she took another bite, though, the subject of Sam brought to mind his, well, whatever it was that was bothering him. She had to admit how much she still struggled with asking for help. She didn't want people to doubt her ability in raising these kids. She also didn't want them to think she was complaining.

"Do you know what you're getting Sam for his birthday?" Melody asked, her large blue eyes peering over the top of her coffee mug as she took a sip.

"Who knows? I was used to sending money to California for him to buy what he wished. But I don't want to do that now. I know if I gave him a couple of twenties in a card that he'd end up spending it on his car."

"Well, that doesn't seem too bad to me. Boys love their cars." Melody set her coffee mug on the table.

"The car isn't the problem. The problem is that even after more money is poured into it I have a feeling that thing still won't—"

The chime of the bell on the door interrupted Charlotte's words. She glanced up to see her longtime friend Hannah hurriedly entering. Hannah wore a brown corduroy work jacket similar in style to the one Charlotte wore. Like her, Charlotte knew Hannah had a larger, nicer parka in her closet, but also like her, it seemed silly to dress up and look all fancy for a quick trip to town.

"Did someone plan a girlfriend party and forget to invite me?" Hannah asked, walking over with her arms wide, giving Charlotte a quick hug.

Hannah's hands were cold, and Charlotte took them

between her own and rubbed them together. Then Charlotte scooted over and patted the bench beside her. Without asking, Melody retrieved another cinnamon roll and another cup of coffee.

Once the pastries were placed on the table, Charlotte knew she needed to step out of her comfort zone. If she didn't take this chance, she might not get another one soon.

Charlotte blew out a breath. "On cold days like this nothing beats a hot cup of coffee, a tasty treat, and some advice."

"Advice?" The word caught Melody's attention. Hannah too glanced over at Charlotte.

"Ladies, I can beat around the bush, or I can just spill it. Sam's been acting very moody lately, withdrawing from the rest of us, and I'm not sure what to do."

She let out another slow breath, thankful she'd gotten it out. For too many days over the past months she'd held everything inside, letting it burden her down like a million bricks. At least now her friends would be able to help.

"He's withdrawing, huh?" Melody rose to grab a little pitcher of cream for Hannah's coffee. "Maybe it's the winter weather—I know I get gloomy this time of year. Or maybe he's just going through another phase of missing his mom. Or maybe it's a combination of both. Everything this year has been new for him. He's probably thinking about what things would be like if he were still in San Diego." Melody pointed her chin toward the window where a scattering of snowflakes were starting to blow downward. "I would bet it's nothing like this."

"And sometimes we can get so focused on what we don't have that we forget about what we do have," Hannah commented. "Like that episode of *Gilligan's Island* when Gilligan found that he had a winning sweepstakes ticket in his pocket. A ticket he couldn't cash in—can you imagine the bad luck of that?"

Charlotte nodded, trying to figure out how Hannah's analogy applied. After a long pause, she finally sighed. "Yes, but unlike Gilligan, who couldn't leave the island, all Sam has to do is cash it in. I wish he realized how much we love him. Even if we don't know how to show it sometimes . . ." Charlotte let her voice trail off.

"Or maybe it's more than that. Maybe it's Valentine's Day," Melody said, adding cream to Hannah's cup—just the right amount. The gesture made Charlotte realize that little details did matter to her friends.

"For some, Valentine's Day is the greatest holiday in the world, and for others it just plain stinks," Melody added. "I can't imagine not having someone to share such a romantic day with."

Charlotte nodded and smiled, but she knew that wasn't Sam's problem. He didn't care about Valentine's Day. Most boys didn't. No, there was more going on inside his head than wishing he had a girlfriend. Much more.

The front door bell jingled again. Melody's head waitress, Ginny, walked in.

Melody offered Ginny a wave, then leaned toward her friends to resume where she'd left off. "Take that flower fundraiser as an example. I can't believe the school still carries on that tradition. Maybe because we're all romantics at heart?"

"Not that true love is found too often in high school," Charlotte said, slightly disappointed that the conversation had already turned away from Sam.

"Sometimes it is. Remember Bonnie and Chuck Greene, who got married right after high school? I think they were in Bill's class. Well, she didn't even know he liked her until she received a rose and a note from him during the fundraiser. I got a card from them just last Christmas and they're still happily married with five or six kids."

"Oh, yes, and the youngest Scott girl too," Hannah added. "Remember the one who worked part time at Fabrics and Fun? I was invited to their wedding last summer, and they talked about that flower fundraiser in the ceremony. Said it was the thing that brought them together."

A chuckle burst from Melody's lips, and Hannah's nose scrunched up as if she was trying to figure out what the woman was laughing about. Melody patted Hannah's hand. "I'm sorry. I wasn't laughing at you. I just remembered when I was in school and the big fight broke out between Pete and Denise. I mean *big*. Do you remember that, Charlotte?"

Charlotte furrowed her brow and tried to think back. She remembered many, many fights—mostly with Denise—but she couldn't specifically remember one that had to do with flowers. "Well, maybe. Why don't you remind me."

The phone rang and Melody turned to Ginny. "Can you get that? I just have to tell one more story."

Ginny nodded unenthusiastically and answered the phone: "Mel's Place, how can I help you?"

"Yes, surely you remember," Melody patted Charlotte's hand. "I think it was Denise's junior year, and Pete was just a freshman. Well, during the flower fundraiser Pete got more flowers than she did. Pete teased her, as only Pete can, and Denise paid him back by supergluing his locker shut. It took the custodian the rest of the day to figure out how to get it opened."

Suddenly a memory fluttered back as Charlotte remembered the phone call she'd received.

"Oh, yes, I remember. The principal called, and Denise got a half-day suspension. She also had to use some of her savings to pay for the cost of fixing the locker. The consequences could have been worse, but the principal said he was going light because they were brother and sister."

Melody laughed and shook her head, her eyes twinkling as the memory replayed in her mind. "It wasn't right, of course, but you should have seen Pete's face when he pulled and pulled on that locker and it didn't budge."

"I don't know what would happen these days if the same situation happened with Sam and Emily." Charlotte tried to turn the conversation back to Sam's struggles. "And it could—or at least something like it," she quickly added. "Like I was saying, these days Sam—"

"Melody?" Ginny called from across the room, interrupting Charlotte. "That was Martha—she needs to add some extra pastries for the tea you're catering today because she got some last minute RSVPs."

"The tea!" Melody jumped up and glanced at the clock. "Where has the morning gone?" She hurried toward Ginny. "Sure, not a problem. I'll throw in a few more scones." She hustled around the display case.

"Speaking of running, I need to go too." Hannah rose. "Frank has a nasty cold and sent me in to town for some medicine. I just came in to pick up a sticky bun to cheer my poor hubby up."

She bent down and gave Charlotte a quick hug. "It was

nice seeing you though. I'll call you later." And with one last wave she hurried out the door. Charlotte considered chasing after her, reminding Hannah she'd forgotten the pastry for Frank, but decided maybe she'd just take one by their house herself. The day outside the window looked too cold to rush into.

As Melody chatted with Ginny about the daily specials, Ginny rewiped the display case Melody had just cleaned.

Charlotte turned her attention to the paper hearts fluttering overhead and tried to remember just what did happen between Pete and Denise after that incident. It was little things like that she wished she'd taken more time to connect with Denise about. Denise no doubt had gotten a lecture from Bob and maybe a few more chores.

And what was my response? Did I ground Denise? Excuse her behavior? Punish Pete? Charlotte honestly couldn't remember.

Charlotte wondered if she ever considered asking her daughter what was going on in her heart. Obviously the flowers had meant much more to Denise than just a simple gift. It could have been a hint that Denise was seeking the love and attention of the guys in her class. And maybe, if Charlotte would have taken the time to talk to her about the desires in the heart of every young woman and the importance of waiting on the Lord for the perfect man, then Denise wouldn't have gotten so wrapped up with Kevin Slater. Maybe so much pain, heartache, and loss could have been prevented.

Charlotte glanced down at her coffee, realizing it was cold. She quickly finished her cinnamon roll and grabbed her purse. She asked Ginny to box up another cinnamon roll for Bob and one for Frank, then she paid for her purchases.

She waved to Melody, who was preparing the pastries for the tea, as she headed toward the door. Charlotte paused, taking in the cold world and wishing that she had one of those car starter gizmos that she'd seen around town. With the push of a button she could start the car and have it warm up. The fact was she'd be halfway home before she'd feel any heat coming out of the car's heater.

With a sigh she buttoned her coat to her chin and hurried to her car. As she fumbled for her keys, it occurred to her that she was perhaps seeing the past through the wrong eyes. She had long ago realized that things happened for a reason. Perhaps she should quit looking back at those times with such regret. Sure they'd been difficult, but if things hadn't happened that way she wouldn't have Sam, Emily, and Christopher with her now. And even though it had been less than a year since they arrived at the farm, her heart skipped a beat at the thought of not having them around.

Chapter
Three

Toby greeted Charlotte with a wag of her tail and a welcome bark. Charlotte climbed from her car and petted the dog's head, noting the cold puffs of air coming from her nose. "C'mon, girl. Let's get inside out of this chill." She spotted lights in the barn as she hurried to the house. It could be Bob—finding a quiet place to escape from Pete. Or vice versa.

She entered the house and relaxed a bit as the warm air enveloped her. That was one good thing about winter— having someplace cozy to return to.

Bob sat at the dining room table reading the paper. His reading glasses were perched on his nose and for the briefest moment he looked like his father sitting there. Pa Stevenson had slouched over his newspaper, sipping on lukewarm coffee in the same serious way—as if he were reading top secret information from the Pentagon rather than the latest news of Bedford, Nebraska.

Charlotte approached and gave him a quick peck on the cheek. "I'm thinking of making baked chicken with cornbread for supper. Doesn't that sound good?"

"Uh-huh," he said without glancing up.

She sat across from him. "You should have seen Christopher's science project. I stayed around a few extra minutes for his presentation. He's a smart one, that kid is. Reminds me of Bill at that age."

Bob nodded, but this time there was no comment.

Charlotte threaded her fingers together and rested her hands on her chin. "So, on the way to school Sam talked me into buying a new vehicle for him. I was thinking about one of those Hummers we sometimes see in Harding— shouldn't cost more than fifty grand, don't you think?"

A smile curled on her lips as she waited for her words to connect with Bob's brain. He quickly glanced up and then noticed her smirk.

"I'm listening. I'm listening. I can't read and talk at the same time, you know. Unlike some people."

"Is that Pete out in the barn?"

Bob shrugged. "Yeah, I suppose. He mumbled something about looking for seed catalogs before he left."

"Oh, did he get that list I left on the counter for him? I hope so. He always finds a better deal than what I can get."

Bob shrugged. "Suppose so. Can't keep track of everyone and everything around here . . ." Bob let his voice trail off, then he flipped the page of the newspaper.

"I know." She rose and squeezed his arm. She glanced toward the kitchen and eyed the counter "I don't see the list up there so I assume he got it. And I won't bother your reading. I think I'll head out and talk to Pete and see if I put yellow squash on the list. The kids kept interrupting me last night, and I'm not sure what ended up on it."

She rebundled herself and patted Toby's head as they ventured out into the cold once more. "It doesn't matter if it's ninety or zero to you, does it, girl." Charlotte smiled as the dog trotted by her side.

She pushed open the barn door, and sure enough, there was Pete sitting on a stool under the light, flipping through a seed catalog, mumbling to himself. The pleasant scent of animals and warm hay tickled her nose. It smelled like hard work even in this dormant season.

"Caught you." Charlotte smirked. "You reading aloud to an audience?"

The milk cow and horses pricked up their ears as if they knew Charlotte was talking about them.

"Just reading about the latest and greatest, out of the view of prying eyes." Pete glanced up and pushed his cap back from his forehead. His eyes had the same dejected look that she'd seen in Sam's just a few hours before.

"Prying eyes?"

"Meaning Dad, not you. Can't move a rusty nail around here without him complaining about it."

Charlotte glanced around the barn, taking everything in: the clean hay, the contented animals, and her youngest son sitting on the milking stool, flipping through the seed catalogs. Her order was tucked in the pocket of his flannel shirt.

"I see you found my list. I appreciate you taking the time to put in the order for me."

"Sure thing, just as long as you don't give me a chewing out if I decide to order Stonehead Hybrid cabbage instead of Golden Acre cabbage this year. I'm thinking of trying it." Pete smirked, leaned back against the barn wall, and crossed his arms over his chest. "Man, listen to me. I'm talking about cabbage like some guys talk about cars or motorcycles. It's the small things in life that make all the difference isn't it?" He spread his arms wide. "Pete Stevenson, this is your life."

Charlotte sighed at his snide retort. "Stonehead Hybrid cabbage sounds good. I don't really mind. As long as it grows and tastes good in my cooking."

Pete flipped through the catalog, finding the page with the cabbage. "I mean, look at this, Mom. How can you pick?"

Charlotte tried to ignore the sarcasm in his voice.

Pete pressed his lips together. "It's a hard choice though. They both look good. Would you believe there's fifteen different varieties to choose from?"

She approached and silently read over Pete's shoulder as he flipped through the glossy pages that displayed bright photographs of perfectly round pumpkins, plump tomatoes, and flawless, beautifully arranged pea pods in the same manner as some guys would look at car or firearm magazines.

"They're always improving things, aren't they? Making heartier plants that yield bigger crops—both in the garden and the field." She patted Pete's shoulder. "And better machines to help harvest them quicker."

"Yeah, but they cost a pretty penny too."

Pete flipped the page again. Charlotte pointed to a photograph of Crimson Sweet watermelons. "Hey, those were good. We should order more of those. I think I only had one packet of watermelon seeds on the list, but what do you think of making it two? Sam likes cold watermelon when he comes in from chores. Maybe we should clear a bigger spot and expand the whole garden. I'd like to get the kids more involved this year."

Pete glanced up and nodded, his blue eyes meeting hers. He sat up straighter on the stool. Charlotte could tell from the look on his face that he was already trying to figure out what he would need to do to make the garden bigger. "That's not a bad idea, especially since they eat so much."

Charlotte chuckled. " I can't leave anything in the fridge for five minutes. Otherwise, poof, it's gone."

Pete stroked his chin the way Bob often did—although Charlotte would never tell him that. Pete prided himself on being different from his father. "Yeah, I could bring the tractor in and expand the garden plot. Get some good fertilizer. Pick out the rocks—we can get that done before the first planting, especially if the kids help."

"So do you think we should double up on everything?" Charlotte asked, already picturing herself working alongside the kids, the warm sun overhead and the warm soil sifting between her fingertips.

"Everything but beets. No one really likes them, and you do all that work just to give them away."

"Good point. Was it Emily—Miss Everything-tastes-better-with-salad—who said they tasted like dirt?"

"Yeah, it sounds familiar. She must have got it from her mom because Denise used to say the same thing."

"Really!" Charlotte folded her arms over her bulky jacket and leaned back against the cow's stall. "I don't remember that. In fact, sometimes I wonder if I was even present when you were kids. There seems to be so much lost in the recesses of my mind, never again to be found."

"Yeah, well, maybe because your mind was on other things, bigger things, like helping Dad run the farm and raising us. But, well, I went to school with her, and some of my sister's antics seemed to come straight out of a TV sitcom." Pete chuckled and swung his foot, kicking at the hay that covered the barn floor.

"Speaking of which," Charlotte said, "I was talking to Melody Givens today and she mentioned some drama happening around a flower fundraiser, something about Denise and you fighting because you got more flowers. Do you remember what started it?"

"Remember? How can I forget? I thought Denise was going to knock my head off because of some silly flowers. I suppose in the long run a glued locker wasn't too bad."

"You're kidding." Charlotte grinned.

"No, I'm serious. I got more flowers than she did during that Valentine's fundraiser thing and you'd think I'd just won the lottery or something. She was so jealous. She always wanted to be the center of attention, and there I was, showing her up in front of the whole school." Pete blinked his eyes as he spoke, then he wiped at his face as if pretending there was dust in his eyes rather than a tear.

Charlotte patted his hand. It was the silliest things, really, that overwhelmed her emotions. A commercial that she knew would make Denise laugh or an eighties song on the radio. Big things, like birthdays and Christmas, she could build up her strength for, but it was those little things that tugged at her heartstrings and caught her off guard.

"Humph." Charlotte tried to clear out the emotion mounting in her throat. "So that flower thing really is as serious as everyone makes it out to be? It seems in my day it was just something fun we did for our friends."

"Most people back then didn't make too big a deal about it. Most people besides my sister, that is." He chuckled to himself. "What Denise never did find out is that Dana bought me one flower—but I bought five more for myself."

Charlotte's laughter joined his. "*You* did? You're kidding. Whatever for?"

"It was Bill's idea, actually. He said I could borrow the money. We worked out a deal that he'd pay for the silly flowers, and I'd do his chores for a week. Not only did Denise get mad—which was part of the plan—but Dana got jealous. She thought there was competition, and agreed to go steady with me after that."

The cow gave a low moo, as if scolding Pete for his wicked scheme. Charlotte couldn't help but chuckle and shake her head. The things kids came up with—it was amazing, really. They were resourceful, sneaky, and smart. Way too smart for their own good.

"So, do you think the kids are doing okay?" Charlotte glanced up, looking at the loft filled with hay but not really seeing it.

The question seemed to come out of the blue, but it had been her intention all long to get Pete's input. Anytime she shared her concerns with Bob he would just suggest adding more chores, as if hard work was the correct answer 100 percent of the time. And Hannah and Melody? Charlotte would have liked to agree with her friends and believe that Sam's problem was just missing his mom, mixed with facing the winter glooms.

But what would Pete say? She knew that even though Pete agitated the kids and egged them on, he was also probably the most tuned in to them. Maybe because he was closer to their age. Or because he also often felt like an outcast on the farm, even though most of the work now rested on his shoulders.

"Yeah, Mom. I think the kids are doing fine. School seems to be going okay. Emily doesn't have a boyfriend, which is a bonus. Christopher hasn't been driving any heavy machinery lately."

"And Sam?" Her question hung in the air like a particle of barn dust.

Pete took a minute to answer. "Well, maybe there's

something going on with Sam. I'm not sure. Who knows what's going through his head—worries about girls, concerns about his schoolwork, maybe missing his mom? It must be hard for the kid. This will be the first birthday he's celebrated without her around."

He elbowed Charlotte in the ribs. "Hey, it's almost February 14th. Maybe I should lend him some money for flowers and he could get Emily's goat. I could use someone to do more of the chores, and maybe a date is just what Sam needs."

Charlotte's eyes widened as she pictured such a thing. "Peter Charles, don't you dare. Spring is right around the corner, and we have enough to worry about without the ups and downs of dating drama to distract us."

Pete pursed his lips and nodded. Then he slipped off the stool and tucked his hands into his pockets.

Charlotte hurried to explain. "I'm talking about Sam and Emily dating, not you, of course. I mean, if you and Dana—"

"Yeah, I know. If only it were that easy. I'm trying to do what I can, but I'm so lame about that type of stuff."

"Maybe you should get her some nice flowers."

"If you think it would help. . . ." Pete's eyes held a hint of hope.

"Well, I can tell you this, son. It wouldn't hurt."

"Yeah, maybe you're right." Pete said as he slid the catalog into his pocket.

Charlotte realized that he hadn't really answered her question about Sam, but at least he was opening up to her. For a few brief moments she even got a glimpse about what was going on in *his* head.

It gave her hope for Sam.

Lord, make a way for Sam to be willing to let us in. Whatever it takes, Lord, soften Sam's heart.

∿ Chapter Four

S am blew into his hands to warm them. His fingers felt as if they were being stabbed by a thousand tiny needles. He hated the cold. Hated always feeling half frozen.

"Dude, tell me that you didn't have to deal with ice like this in California. I mean it's like trying to longboard on glass or something." Paul flipped his hair out of his face as he glided next to Sam.

"Or something—" Sam mumbled to himself. Then his voice rose as he called to his friend. "Heck, no, we don't have ice like this, even at Christmas. If I was there right now I'd be wearing shorts and a T-shirt, and zipping down the hills with the ocean air on my face."

"Man, please, give it up. It sounds like you're writing poetry or something." His other friend, Jake, chuckled. He kicked up his skateboard and caught it in his hands.

"I'll show you poetry. Poetry in motion." Sam dodged around a dirty pile of old snow, leaning forward on his board, feeling the cold air hitting his cheeks and numbing his nose.

"So, dude, can you show me that trick you were doing last week?"

Sam looked around and shrugged. "I don't know. It's snowed since then. There's ice all over."

"C'mon, Slater," Jake begged.

"Fine, if you're going to whine like my sister I guess I don't have a choice." Sam skated toward a spot that looked the least icy.

His two friends circled Sam and waited.

Sam cleared his throat. "First you have to learn how to ollie and then you have to learn to nose manual." He dropped his longboard to the ground, then stood on it. "For the ollie nose manual, you want to approach the curb or platform at a medium speed in an ollie stance. Then pop, and go right into the nose manual. From there you pop out, land, and roll away."

Sam could see from his friends' faces that they had no idea what he was talking about. So he bent over and grabbed the board, using big hand motions to show them what it would look like.

"See, the board will pop up and land on the two front wheels," Sam explained, trying to be patient.

Paul and Jake stared at him blankly. Ice or no ice, he'd just have to show them.

"Fine, move out of the way." Sam scanned the parking lot. His favorite platform was covered in a pile of snow, so he pointed his board toward a loading ramp. It was higher than he usually popped onto, but he knew it could work.

He stepped onto his board with an ollie stance, his back foot in the middle of the board and his front foot as close as possible to the front of the board. He kicked off, and just before he reached the platform he put all his weight on his front foot. The effect was supposed to pop the board forward, carrying him up onto the loading dock.

But Sam felt the board slipping backward and his body flying forward. He stretched out his hands to break his fall, but his rib cage hit the edge of the ramp first. Sharp pain shot through his ribs and he felt the wind escaping in one big whoosh.

Sam crumbled to the ground and struggled to catch his breath. He heard his friends' laughter. If he had any strength they'd each get a knuckle sandwich.

"Dude, are you okay?" Jake's voice called out.

Sam heard the pounding of footsteps.

Paul's laughter shook his frame. "I wish I had a video camera. We could have totally won ten thousand dollars from *America's Funniest Videos* with that one! Man, I think you hit black ice. It was righteous."

Righteous? Sam moaned. Where did they get their slang, from twenty-year-old movies? He grabbed his side and winced, knowing his friends from California would never use words like that. Also thinking that a stupid accident like this wouldn't happen back home. There was no black ice there. No—

"Hey, you kids need to get out of here!" A man's voice split the air. It was the produce manager of Herko's Grocery Store waving a broom in Sam's direction. "We don't need you out here getting hurt and worrying our customers. We—we're not going to pay if you break anything either!"

Sam first sat, leaning his back against the concrete platform. Then he tried to turn to one knee.

Paul and Jake sobered and turned toward Sam.

"Sorry, man. I shouldn't have laughed. You okay?" Paul grabbed Sam's board.

Jake attempted to help Sam up. "You didn't break anything, did you?" He grabbed under Sam's arms and pulled, causing another sharp pain to spread through Sam's ribcage.

Sam winced. "Dude, ouch. You're hurting me. I can do it."

"Yeah, that's right. Get along now," the produce manager called again. The man had paused just outside the side door, standing with his shoulders back as if that green apron was a suit of armor. "Don't you see the sign? You know you can't be here," he added with a wave of his finger.

Sam glanced at the sign. He stood up and began to hobble away. "Man, it says no *solicitations*," he muttered. "Bet he doesn't even know what that means. He should go back to school and get a real job."

Paul and Jake walked by Sam's side as they made their way to the school.

"This place is so stupid. If you had any idea what the real world is like, you wouldn't be able to stand it here. You have no idea what you're missing in the world out there," Sam said without looking up, keeping his eyes fixed on the ground, watching for more black ice. "I'm sick of it. All of it. I'm blowin' this joint."

Paul nodded. "Totally, there must be a better place to skate."

"Yeah, how about behind Fabrics and Fun? Isn't that lady your great-grandma or somethin'?" Jake added.

Sam smirked. He wasn't going to try to explain himself— or the fact that he was talking about much more than skateboarding. They'd find out the truth soon enough.

He glanced back at the lame grocery store with the lame guy in the green apron one more time.

They'd all find out.

Chapter Five

Charlotte watched from the window, and it seemed Christopher's feet didn't touch the ground as he propelled himself down the snowy driveway. His red backpack bounced on his back, and Toby bounded toward him, barking. There was nothing as natural as a boy meeting up with his dog at the end of a long day.

Emily lumbered behind Christopher at half speed. Charlotte watched the bus door, waiting for Sam to exit. But when Emily got ten feet away, the doors closed and the yellow bus rumbled off—the one spot of color over the flat, gray horizon.

Christopher's feet pounded up the steps, then the door swung open. A whoosh of cold air swept in along with a smiling boy.

"Guess what, Grandma?" Christopher slid his shoes off and then his socks, leaving them on the soggy mat as he padded into the kitchen with bare feet.

"Let me guess, good news about your science project?" Charlotte set the potato peeler on the bottom of her chipped sink, rinsed off the last potato, placed it on the cutting board, then rinsed off her hands.

"Nah, we're not going to hear about that for a week at least, remember?" His cheeks were red, and he puffed as he slid off his backpack. He unzipped it and handed her a crumpled paper—the same bluish green color that they used to print the cafeteria menus on.

"We have a new school newspaper. It just started up, and in the very first issue they have *my* poem."

"Your poem? Really?" She glanced on the first page and spotted a story about 4-H winter activities and a column written by the eighth-grade class president concerning preparing for high school. Turning the page over, Charlotte spotted a poem about butterflies and flowers. She was just about to ask Christopher if he was sure he had the right paper when she noticed his name at the end of the poem.

"Christopher, did you write—" The squeak of the door opening interrupted Charlotte's words, and Emily clomped inside. She only wore a thin sweater over her shirt despite the new winter coat that hung in her closet upstairs.

"Hold on, Christopher, I need to talk to Emily for a sec."

Emily paused, dropped her purse on the floor, and glanced up as if she were five and had been caught with her hand in the cookie jar.

"Did I, uh, do something wrong?"

"No, at least I don't think you did." Charlotte folded her arms over her chest and gave Emily a fake scowl. Then she winked at her granddaughter. "I was just wondering about Sam. He wasn't on the bus. Did he have to work today?"

Emily shrugged. "I don't think so. He said he was getting a ride home with Jake, but he didn't say why. Maybe they're skateboarding or something."

"In this weather?"

Emily headed upstairs. "I never accused them of having any brains," she called back.

Charlotte pushed worries of Sam out of her mind and turned back to Christopher, noticing a look of expectation and excitement on his face.

"Well, it's a great poem," she said. "Where did you come up with the idea?"

"You mean about the butterflies playing chase through the flowerbed?" Christopher moved to the refrigerator and pulled out the jug of milk then poured himself a glass. He shrugged. "I don't know. It just came to me."

"Really? Is it a common thing to have poems pop up in your head? Or—" Charlotte paused. She had a sinking feeling that Christopher didn't understand what it meant to submit a poem to the school newsletter. Maybe Christopher thought *submit* meant to copy something that he liked. Maybe the teacher hadn't made it clear.

"Christopher, I don't know how to ask this, but—" Charlotte bit her lip.

Christopher turned to her. His eyes were wide with questions. "Yes, Grandma?"

She read the poem again, deciding that maybe it was better if she just let it slide. Christopher was creative. He was a good writer . . . Then again, she couldn't imagine him being interested in flowers and butterflies. It didn't seem typical that a ten-year-old boy would want to write about *that*.

Charlotte approached where Christopher was standing and leaned back against the counter. "So, what were the guidelines for submitting a piece to the paper?"

"Guidelines?" Christopher scratched the top of his blond head.

"Yes, you know, the rules. Did the teacher give you rules on what to turn in—or what not to turn in?"

"Um, it had to be something we wrote. I'd get in trouble if I copied something—" He took a big drink of his milk. The glass covered his face, and when he lowered it any hint of excitement was gone.

"But you just said a minute ago that you were supposed to write about something that you are interested in."

"I thought about that." Christopher scratched his chin in a way that reminded Charlotte of Pete—and of Bob.

Charlotte hid her smile. "And, what were you thinking?"

"Well, I like spaceships and tornados and stuff like that. But all the editors are girls."

"So?"

He lifted a finger into the air. "So, I thought I'd send in something that would interest *them*."

Charlotte read the poem again. "And you realized girls like flowers and butterflies and knew your best shot to get in was to write about that?"

Christopher glanced around the kitchen. He pursed his lips and nodded. "Yeah, pretty much." Then he grabbed an apple off the counter, took a big bite, and headed up the stairs. "And if you don't believe I wrote it, I can prove it."

"Oh, I believe you—I'm just surprised." Charlotte had a sinking feeling in the pit of her stomach. She felt bad. She hadn't meant to accuse her grandson.

Christopher called from the stairs. "Hold on!"

Thirty seconds later he jogged back down with a half-dozen wadded-up pieces of paper in his hands.

"These were under my bed." He had a shy look on his face. "I, uh, kind of stuffed them under there the last time I cleaned my room." He unwadded them and spread them on the table. Charlotte glanced at them, and sure enough, they were various stages of the poem, from first attempts to the finished piece.

"Wow, I'm impressed. When did you get so smart?"

"Gee, Grandma, don't sound so surprised."

"I didn't mean it like that. The poem is so good—I'm just amazed!" She patted his cheek. "But I do think you're *too* smart for your own good. And too young to be thinking about girls and poetry."

"Yeah, well, I'm not thinking about them like *that*. Ick!" He grabbed the newspaper and hurried upstairs. "Emily, look!"

Charlotte chuckled to herself, remembering when Pete was that age, and she realized that Christopher would be thinking about girls in *that way* before she knew it.

The side door opened and a whiff of cold air blew in. Bob's cheeks were red. He shut the door behind him and then rubbed his hands together. Even though it was below freezing outside, he wore his overalls and plaid shirt without a coat.

Charlotte wrinkled her nose at him, and she could tell from the guilty look on his face that he expected a lecture.

"Just going between here and the barn," Bob mumbled under his breath. "No use getting all suited up for that."

Charlotte was just about to reply when she heard the sound of a vehicle coming down the driveway. It sounded like it had a broken muffler—or maybe was hiding a jet engine underneath the hood. The roar seemed to rattle the windows. Before she could open her mouth to complain, Bob stalked out the door.

She hurried to the window and watched as Sam slowly climbed out of the passenger side of the car. From his awkward movements, she could tell he was injured. She considered running out to see what was wrong, but Bob was already busy talking to Sam's friend Jake.

From Bob's hand motions, she guessed that Bob was telling the youth that he needed to get his car checked out. As if Jake didn't know that already.

Sam didn't stick around to listen to his grandpa's mechanical advice. Instead, he tucked his skateboard under his arm and walked stiffly to the house. From the look on his face, she could tell Sam was trying to hold his emotion in. Whether it was tears, or harsh words, she couldn't tell.

Sam kicked the door open. It took every ounce of willpower not to hurry over to him. Charlotte lifted her chin, eyeing his ripped shirt underneath the jacket he was struggling to take off. "You okay?"

Sam's lower lip quivered, and the look in his eyes reminded Charlotte of the little boy he used to be.

"Fine."

"Did you fall?"

He shrugged. "I've done that trick a hundred times." He mumbled something Charlotte didn't understand. Then his voice rose. "Man, I hate this ice." He held his side as he moved through the kitchen.

"Did you hit the ground?"

"No. The edge of a cement ramp."

"May I look?"

"I'm fine, Grandma," he said.

Still, she moved toward him, and he leaned his skateboard against the wall at the bottom of the stairs.

Charlotte lifted his shirt and noticed a large bruise forming on his rib cage. She tried not to show her anxiety. "Your ribs could be broken, Sam. We should see the doctor."

"And what's he going to do, wrap them? Tell me to take things easy?"

"Maybe tell you no more skating in winter. With all the black ice out there you're lucky if it's only a few cracked ribs. You could have really gotten hurt."

Charlotte's words were interrupted by the door opening and Bob marching in, finger pointed. In three long strides he reached Sam.

"You need to tell your friends that if they want you to ride with them, they best take better care of their cars. Did you hear that knocking in the engine? The car could break down in the middle of nowhere. There are some places you'd have to hike for a few miles to get help, and in the cold, well, hypothermia shouldn't be messed with."

Sam dropped his shirt. His face immediately transformed from pain to anger. "Don't you think I know that?"

Sam turned and stomped up the stairs. "I'm the one who's always complaining that we live in the middle of nowhere. The Arctic has to be warmer and more populated than Bedford. Who would even choose to live in this place? People who don't know any better, that's who."

At the top of the stairs he headed into his room, slamming his door.

"Well, I never . . ." Bob crossed his arms over his broad chest. "What's got into him? These kids have no understanding of the dangers out there."

Charlotte turned and moved back to the sink, taking out a cutting board and knife, trying to figure out the best way to calm her husband without being disrespectful herself. She grabbed a few potatoes out of the bin.

"Yes, that's true. Sam's friend doesn't need to be driving a car that could break down any moment. It's harsh weather out there."

"I wasn't talking about Sam's friend. I'm talking about Sam." Bob moved to the dining room table and picked up the ag report. He stared at the page, but she could tell he really wasn't reading it.

The knife clicked, clicked, clicked against the chopping board as she cubed the potatoes and tossed them into the stockpot on the stovetop. "Did you notice how banged up he was?"

"Who?" Bob mumbled, turning the page.

"Sam. He fell skateboarding. Said he hit the edge of a concrete ramp. He must have hit hard too, because there's a nasty bruise. I wouldn't be surprised if he has a few broken ribs."

"Humph." Bob folded the paper and placed it on the table. "It's plumb foolishness to be riding that board this time of year as it is."

"Yes, that's true, but maybe you should look at his injury."

"Me?" Bob readjusted his John Deere cap on his head. "Why me?"

"Well, you're the one who figured out Pete's arm was broken that one time, and not just sprained. I agree that Sam does do a lot of foolish things, but that doesn't mean we let him suffer when he's injured."

Bob rose and moved to his recliner. "Well, if Sam wants me

to, then I can look at it. But you have to remember he's a teenage boy, Charlotte. Teenage boys goof around. They get hurt. Sam doesn't need to be coddled." Then Bob clicked on the television, which made it clear he was done with the conversation.

CHARLOTTE SCOOPED fluffy mashed potatoes onto each plate and then topped them with brown gravy as she glanced from Bob, to Sam, to Christopher, to Emily.

"So anyone got anything exciting to share about their day?" She offered chicken to Bob, ignoring Emily's upturned nose as she passed the plates.

"Yeah, I'm a published writer." Christopher pulled the school newspaper from his back pocket and waved it in the air.

Christopher handed it to Emily. Her face brightened as she read it. "Ah, I think it's cute. I like that. It sounds like a greeting card or something."

Sam swiped it out of his sister's hands.

"Let me see that."

"Sam, that wasn't nice." Charlotte plopped a piece of chicken on her oldest grandson's plate.

"Let me see it *please*," Sam said as he opened the paper.

"Back page. On the bottom."

Sam turned the paper over and snorted. "Do you mean this sissy poem? You've got to be kidding."

"Yeah, well, it got published, didn't it?" Christopher jutted out his chin.

"Enough." Bob put down his fork with a thunk.

"Did you read it?" Sam tossed the newspaper in Bob's direction, and it landed just an inch shy of Bob's plate.

"Hey," Christopher protested, his voice wavering. "You're gonna get gravy on it, Sam. Be careful."

"Guys can write about flowers, Sam," Emily interjected. "And butterflies *are* insects. Right, Grandma?"

Charlotte nodded her answer, but her eyes weren't focused on her granddaughter. Instead, she watched Bob. Charlotte could tell from the look in Bob's eye that Sam was about to lose his dinner privileges. She put down her fork and quickly tried to think of a way to change the tide of the conversation.

"Speaking of flowers, Emily, are you going to be buying a flower for anyone? The fundraiser is coming up quick."

Emily tucked a stand of blonde hair behind her ear. "Weren't you the one who told me that dating at my age wasn't a good idea?"

Charlotte wiped her mouth with her napkin. "I wasn't encouraging you to date. I just thought maybe you'd like to give one to a friend. Like Ashley."

"Grandma," Emily's blue eyes widened. "I don't want to waste five dollars giving my friend a flower. I'm saving up for some new shoes, remember? Besides, it's totally lame when someone gives someone else a flower just because they're friends."

"Oh, I'm not sure," Charlotte glanced at Emily. "I've gotten flowers from my friends before, and I like it. It's a nice reminder that someone is thinking about me."

"Speaking of friends," Sam said, sitting up straighter in his chair. He kept his eyes on his plate though. "I've been asked to stay over at Paul's house next Friday night—a week from tomorrow. I hope it's okay for me to go."

He glanced at Bob, and then to Charlotte, holding her gaze. The hardness of his look softened. "Maybe hanging out and playing the Wii might help, you know, cheer me up."

Sam's eyes locked with Charlotte's and they looked hopeful.

"Does Paul have Super Karate Fight Machine 2?" Christopher stuck his feet under his bottom and leaned on the table. "I heard that's the best."

"Chris, even if he did, it has a T rating, and besides, you're not invited." Sam smirked.

"That's not fair," Christopher whined.

"Christopher," Charlotte said, "Paul is Sam's age. Just like Sam doesn't hang out with your friends, you don't need to hang out with his. Did you say Friday, Sam?"

"Yeah, we're just going to chill. Do guy stuff, you know." Sam leaned back from the table, wincing slightly as he stretched his arm.

When they finished eating they all waited while Bob pulled out the story Bible. He opened it to his marked spot. "Let's see what encouragement God's Word will bring us today," he said, clearing his throat and looking at each one of them around the table. "Lord knows we need it."

Yes, indeed, Charlotte thought, glancing at Sam out of the corner of her eye. *Maybe a fun birthday and time with his friends will be just what Sam needs to turn him around, to point him to the right path.*

Chapter
Six

Emily sniffed the air as she descended the stairway into the kitchen on Saturday morning. Her grandma was there, peeking into the oven, checking on something she was baking. Something that smelled good.

The last step squeaked slightly as Emily stepped on it, and Charlotte turned. She placed her hand over her heart.

"Oh goodness, you startled me."

"Why so nervous? Is there something I don't know?" Emily made a face, pretending to be shocked.

Charlotte chuckled and placed her hands on her hips. "If you must know, I'm baking a cake—"

"For Sam's birthday, I know."

Emily watched as her grandma pulled a chocolate cake from the oven.

"Do you want to help frost it when it's cool?" Charlotte asked. "Strawberry frosting is his favorite, right? Although I'm quite sure it's the only pink thing your brother likes."

Emily nodded.

She leaned against the counter, watching her grandma work. Emily knew she had to get outside to do her chores, but from the dim gray sky out the window and the wind that rattled the windows, she quickly tried to think of a way to distract her grandmother.

"Grandma, you know I'm completely broke, and I was trying to figure out a way to do something for Sam."

"How about giving him coupons for making his bed? Or putting away his laundry? I think he'd really appreciate that."

"And have to enter his room that smells like dirty socks and sweat?" Emily wrinkled her nose. "No, thanks."

"You could bake him something. Cookies maybe."

Emily crossed her arms over her chest as her eyes darted around the kitchen. They landed on the coat rack by the door. "Actually, I was thinking of making him something." She hurried to the rack and removed three layers of coats and jackets, finding a gray hooded sweatshirt at the bottom of the pile. "Can I use this?"

"I don't understand . . ." Her grandmother pulled out a bag of chocolate chips from the pantry, mumbling to herself that someone had been in them again. "I just bought these things—who keeps getting into the chocolate?"

Emily tried to pretend she didn't hear. She didn't want to have to confess that sometimes her after-school snack was a handful of chocolate chips.

"Uncle Pete hasn't worn this since I've been here—" Emily carried the sweatshirt to her grandmother. "I think I can use it to make something."

"Well maybe. I think I bought it too small."

"With some scissors and a few homemade corduroy patches from my old skirt, I could make it look cool."

"It seems odd that you'd take a new sweatshirt and tear it up, but I suppose if Pete's not wearing it . . ."

"Cool. Can I use it then?"

"First, you've got to check with Pete. And second, you have to do your chores."

"But it's—"

"Cold out there, I know. How 'bout I make some cocoa for you. It will be ready by the time you get back."

"Okay. If I must." Emily trudged over to the back door and slid on her boots. Then she put on her thick Cornhuskers sweatshirt, followed by her thickest jacket, gloves, and stocking cap, knowing that she'd still freeze, no matter how many layers she put on.

The wind bit at her nose, causing it to sting. She hurried forward, but not too fast as to slip on the icy snow.

In the movies she always saw snow falling as soft flakes from the sky. She imagined it equally fluffy on the ground, almost like ice cream that your boots would sink into. Instead, the snow here was icy from the few days it had warmed above freezing, melted slightly, and then frozen again. It was also dirty. Nothing like they showed on TV.

With numb hands, she tugged on the barn door and then slipped inside, shutting the door soundly behind her. The light was on, and she could see Uncle Pete up ahead, milking Trudy.

"Hey, Uncle Pete."

"Hey yourself."

"I have a question for you."

Pete glanced at her over his shoulder and paused in his milking. "Whatever it is, the answer is no."

"Uncle Pete." Emily gently slugged his arm. "You haven't even heard it yet."

"Well, if it involves driving you somewhere, helping you do something, or pulling out my wallet, the answer is no."

"Haha. It's none of those." Emily crossed her arms over her chest. "So I guess the answer is yes."

"What is it?" His hands moved in a steady rhythm as he continued milking. The milk was white and thick, and Emily liked the way it made a steady rhythm as it splashed into the bucket. Before living on the farm she'd never given much thought to milking, or cows, or where her food came from. Now she couldn't help but think of it whenever she went to the store, amazed that so many things worked together to put food on the shelves.

"Well . . . I was wondering if I could have your gray sweatshirt."

"Sweatshirt?"

"Yeah, on the coat rack."

"I have a gray sweatshirt on the coat rack?"

"Obviously if you can't remember, then you don't need it anymore."

"Oh, yeah, I think I got that for my last birthday, although I don't remember who from. What are you gonna do with it?"

"I'm gonna fix it up for Sam. Make it look like a skater sweatshirt."

"Fix it up, huh? Well, I'm looking forward to seeing that."

"Thanks, Uncle Pete." Emily threw her arms around his back and offered a quick squeeze.

With that taken care of, she quickly hurried down to the horse stalls. "How are my pretty girls today?" Stormy perked her ears, and Emily rubbed her muzzle. It was warm and soft, and Stormy pressed her head forward for more attention, just like Toby sometimes nuzzled up to Christopher's leg.

The truth was that Emily would have tried to do something

nice for Sam even if it wasn't his birthday. He'd been grumpy lately—really grumpy. And more than that, he'd been acting strange too. She thought back to the last couple of days when she'd actually found him cleaning his room not once, but twice. Then there were his cutting remarks. The things he mumbled under his breath. Things he thought no one else had heard. Complaints about the farm, and about *blowing this joint*. Hearing those things and seeing the lost look in her brother's eyes made Emily's stomach hurt so much that she wanted to throw up.

Emily scooped up the grain from the feed barrel and filled the horses' feed bin. Along with the sick feeling in her stomach, she had a sad feeling too. She felt bad for Sam that it was his first birthday without Mom. She knew her turn was coming soon, but he had to face it first, and she wondered what type of messed-up feelings were going on in his head.

And as much as she argued with her brother, she hated to see him so grouchy, because it just made everyone else cranky around him.

Emily finished up with the horses. Next up was feeding the chickens, which wasn't that much fun since they didn't lay many eggs this time of year.

Pete had finished milking and was now mucking the stalls, lost in thought. He didn't even turn as she approached.

"Thinking about Dana?" Emily asked as she passed by.

From the red that rose to his cheeks, Emily knew he was.

"What? No," Pete stammered.

"It's okay, Uncle Pete. I like her too. And with Valentine's Day coming up it's the perfect time to show her how much you care." Emily tucked her gloved hands into her jacket pockets.

"Listen to you. You sound like some sappy television commercial."

"I may be sappy, but I'm a girl. And I know what girls like, and on Valentine's Day they like—"

"Yeah, yeah, yeah." Pete returned to his work. "I know, I'll do something. It's Grandpa you need to worry about."

"Grandpa?"

"Yeah. Your grandmother is lucky if she receives a kiss on the cheek. In fact, I can't remember him *ever* buying her a card, let alone doing anything mushy."

"Really? No flowers? No chocolate, nothing?" Emily rubbed her nose with her glove and noticed it smelled like Stormy.

"Not that I can remember. I think he's been too busy taking care of the farm to think about stuff like that."

"Well, that's just wrong. Doesn't he know how happy it would make Grandma?"

Pete shrugged. "If you say so."

"Men! They're all alike. Seriously, Grandpa so needs help . . ."

Emily tapped the side of her head. "*Hmm*. That gives me an idea."

Chapter Seven

Charlotte felt butterflies of excitement dance around her stomach on the drive home from church. Pete had made a dozen excuses why he wasn't attending church, so instead Charlotte put him to work getting things ready for Sam's birthday. It made sense to celebrate on Sunday when they could all take the time to be together, rather than Tuesday when they would all be busy. She'd baked the cake the day prior and had kept it hidden in Pete's apartment above the tractor shed.

She'd also done the preparation for BLTs and had hidden them in the back of the fridge. She'd splurged on those expensive Doritos chips and Dr. Pepper that Sam liked so much. She'd made it as easy as possible for Pete to get everything ready.

Charlotte was imagining a fun family afternoon as they parked the car and strolled inside. She held her breath as she entered the house, expecting to see the cake and presents on the table. But when she scanned the kitchen, her heart sank to see everything was exactly like they'd left it, including the pile of dirty cereal bowls stacked by the sink.

"Pete!" she called, partly from frustration and partly

from worry. Had there been an emergency while she was gone? "Pete!"

Pete jumped from the couch in one fluid motion, and she could tell by his wild eyes he was half asleep.

"Oh, dang," he mumbled, wiping his eyes and meeting Charlotte's irritated gaze. Then, noticing Sam behind Charlotte, he held up one finger. "Sam, close your eyes."

Sam sauntered over to the dining room table and sat. Bob sat beside him, seeming perfectly content to watch Charlotte hustle around to put everything together.

Sam lowered his head on his arms and closed his eyes, not appearing the least bit excited. Charlotte got the chips out of the pantry and the soda and BLT fixings from the fridge while Pete ran to his apartment for the cake.

Emily ran for the presents. "Get excited, Sam. It's your birthday!"

"Wow, Sam. You're almost an adult," Christopher said as he counted the unlit candles on the cake Pete carried in.

Finally, everything was set up.

"Okay, open your eyes." Pete tapped his shoulder.

Sam sat up and opened them.

"Surprise!" Pete, Emily, Christopher, and Charlotte chimed in unison.

"Surprise." Bob added with a sly grin.

"Look, chocolate cake with homemade strawberry frosting, just like Mom used to make," Emily said, sneaking a clump of frosting off the plate.

Sam nodded and forced a smile.

"I was wondering if that was a tradition." Charlotte placed plates on the table. "I remember visiting your mom when Sam was just two. I was both pleased and surprised when she made this cake. It's an old family recipe."

"Why were you surprised?" Emily asked, making a lettuce and tomato sandwich. Charlotte wondered if she'd ever grow out of her vegetarian stage.

"Well, growing up, she always complained about helping me in the kitchen. She didn't think it was fair that she had to help me cook and bake when Pete and Bill got to work outside."

"So she liked outside chores better?" Christopher asked.

"No, not really. But at least outside she didn't have my eyes constantly watching her. Or so she said." Charlotte chuckled. She was thankful that they could talk about Denise in such an easy manner. It had been hard for so many months not mentioning her or her accident even though she was in the forefront of everyone's mind.

After lunch, Sam opened an envelope with a small wad of cash. He looked to Charlotte for an explanation.

"Gas money." Charlotte grinned.

"But my car's broken down."

"Actually," said Pete, "I was tinkering with it this morning, before I took that little nap on the couch, and I think I found the problem. I just need to call Brad in the morning and order a part. Should be able to get it up and running by Wednesday."

"Cool." Sam smiled and then reached for more bacon for another sandwich.

Without a word, Emily and Christopher went upstairs. A minute later Emily returned with a package wrapped in what appeared to be a paper bag that she had decorated with markers. Christopher's wrapping—a plastic grocery bag—was a little less sophisticated.

"Hey, you're not finished opening your presents yet." Emily handed her gift to Sam.

He opened it to find the skater's hoodie. "Hey, thanks, Em."

"Do you like it? I tried to make it just like one of those in your skater magazine, but it's actually one of Uncle Pete's old sweatshirts that Grandma helped me grunge out." Sam nodded, but didn't seem overly enthusiastic.

Next he opened a soccer ball from Pete, and a book on Tony Hawk from Christopher. The wrappings fell to the floor, providing Lightning, Christopher's cat, with something new to play with.

"Found it at the library's used-book sale," Christopher said between bites of cake.

"Thanks, guys." Sam rose.

"Not so fast." Bob pulled his worn leather wallet from his back pocket, and took out two slips of paper, tossing them across the table to Sam.

"What's that?"

"Tickets to the snowmobile races up in Harding. They're happening next Sunday. Good seats too."

"Cool. Maybe Paul could stay over and we could go together." Sam turned to Charlotte. "Grandma, do you think we could borrow your car to go up? It's more reliable."

"I don't think that's what your grandfather had in mind, Sam." Charlotte glanced at Bob and noticed his shoulders sink. She'd been surprised when he'd come home with the tickets, announcing that he thought some one-on-one time with his grandson was just what was needed. Obviously, Sam didn't feel the same.

"Well, if I can't take Paul, how about Jake?"

It was Pete who punched Sam's arm.

"Hello . . . earth to Sam. Will you take a sec and think about who got those tickets for you?"

Sam's eyebrows lifted in surprise, then he turned to his grandfather. Charlotte turned too and noticed Bob's face turning slightly red.

"Oh, yeah." Sam tossed his hair back from his forehead. "I, uh, didn't realize you liked snowmobile races, Grandpa."

Bob shrugged. "I haven't always been so old and cranky. There were times I actually liked to have fun. I even raced myself once or twice."

"Sure, then. We can go—" Sam's face fell, and Charlotte assumed it was because he realized the event fell on the same day he would still be with his friends. "I guess we'll plan on that for Sunday."

Bob nodded, but the excitement over his gift had all but faded.

"One more gift." Charlotte handed him a box she'd wrapped herself. She sucked in a slow breath suddenly feeling foolish for her choice. After all, if Sam didn't appreciate tickets to go see snowmobile races she knew there would be far less enthusiasm over her gift.

Sam slowly opened it as if he was worried about what was inside.

"Looks like a book," Emily said, peering over his shoulder.

"Yeah, that's what I'm worried about," Sam said sarcastically.

He opened it to find a Bible. "Cool. It has my name on it," he said as he ran his finger over the gold letters.

"There's more." Charlotte felt her throat growing tight with emotion. "Look inside." She found this last gift late last night when she'd been going through a box of old letters in the closet. Bob had called her sentimental for hanging on to too many things over the years, but she was glad she had. It was good to remember, to look back, and to consider how God brought their family through those trials. To remember that he would bring them through the ones to come.

Sam opened the Bible and lifted out a letter addressed to Bob and Charlotte. "What's this?" Then his jaw dropped when he looked first to the return address and then to the postmark.

"It's a letter from your mom. It's the first one she wrote to us after your birth. I thought you'd like to read it."

"Wow—okay," he said softly as he stuffed it back into the Bible and then pushed the Bible to the table, standing carefully, favoring his side.

Charlotte searched his face, looking for disappointment, but instead she noticed his lids rimming with tears.

Sam quickly looked away, not willing to show his emotions. He wiped his face and then turned to leave.

Bob grabbed his arm. "Hold on, mister."

"What?"

"Don't you have something to say to your family—like thank you? Everyone has put a lot of thought into your gifts. They took time to consider what you'd like. Everyone sacrificed to make this day special. You should show some appreciation."

Sam stared at his feet. "You're right. Sorry, Grandpa. Thanks again, everyone." His voice sounded scratchy, full of emotion, and Charlotte realized she should have given Sam the letter another time—when he wasn't surrounded by people.

Think, Charlotte! Think next time. The last thing Sam wants is to be caught getting teared up over missing his mom.

Sam shoved his hands in his pockets and his tone changed, as if he was pushing down the emotion. As if he was purposefully putting up a wall between himself and the rest of his family. "Everything is just great," he said flatly.

Sam slumped back into the dining room chair, as if resigning himself to sitting out the rest of his party, and began thumbing through the book on Tony Hawk.

"Hey, Grandma, did I tell you that there's going to be another writing contest in the school paper?" Christopher chatted, oblivious to the underlying tension in the room.

"No, really? Tell me about it."

"Well . . ." Christopher smiled, enjoying the attention. "We have to turn in stories two weeks from now. There's a fifty-dollar prize for the best true story, and a twenty-five-dollar prize for the best fiction story. I've been thinking about writing one."

Charlotte rose and began clearing the lunch dishes. "That's a lot of money. It sounds like something worthwhile."

"Yeah, I think I'm going to try."

"Just as long as you don't write about rainbows and flowers again," Sam mumbled.

"So, are you going to write fiction or nonfiction?" Pete asked, taking a chunk of cake off the cake plate with his fingers.

"Is nonfiction the true story?" Christopher asked, scratching his head.

Pete nodded.

"Yeah, that's the one. It's more money. What do you think, Grandma?"

Charlotte was only half listening to Christopher. Instead, her thoughts were focused on Sam. "Good idea," Charlotte said. "You should try."

Sam sat there in the chair looking as if he were in a room full of strangers. He had a hesitant look on his face—as if he was worried. What was going on in his head?

Charlotte carried a stack of dishes next to the sink and began rinsing each one, placing them in the dishwasher. She realized that, for the most part, Sam merely tolerated life on the farm—as if he was just biding his time. But was there something else going on?

"Here you go; here's the last of it." Emily handed her grandma the last dirty plate.

Charlotte's shoulders and back ached as she finished loading the dishwasher. Lost in thought, she rinsed out the washcloth and wiped off the dining room table, finally realizing that everyone had slipped away and left her to clean up alone. It hadn't changed much since her own kids were teens. Bob, Denise, and Pete always wanted to do their own thing rather than spend time together.

"Is this what family is about?" Charlotte mumbled as she wiped the crumbs from the table into her hand. Somehow she expected more . . . wanted more.

BOB WAS IN A SOUR MOOD as he prepared for bed. Charlotte ran a brush through her short brown hair, which seemed to be getting grayer by the day, and turned to him.

"It's hard for him, you know."

"Hard for who?"

"Sam. This is his first birthday without his mom. That's hard. They had their own way of doing things, their own traditions. I know he misses her."

"We all miss her, Charlotte." Bob put his toothbrush in the holder.

"Yes, I know, but it's different for the kids." She set her brush on the dresser. "Maybe I made a mistake by making that cake. Did you notice? Sam didn't even have a piece. I was just trying to give him something familiar, but maybe it was just more of a reminder that his mom isn't here—and never will be."

She padded over to their bed, the cold floor causing her toes to curl as she walked. Then she slid off her warm bathrobe and slipped between the cold sheets. A small shiver ran down her spine.

"It's hard knowing what to do, you know? Or what not to do. It's not like there's a manual or anything to follow. Nothing could have prepared any of us for this."

Bob climbed into bed and then flipped off the small lamp on the night table. Charlotte felt a wall go up between them. Her mind bounded from Sam, to Emily and the flower fundraiser, to worries about Christopher getting teased about his poem, back to Emily again.

Ten minutes passed and she could tell from his breathing that he wasn't asleep.

"Bob," she whispered in the dark.

"Hmm . . ."

"Can I ask you something?"

"Sure."

"Well, there is this fundraiser at school. Every year the cheerleaders sell flowers. It's a big deal, even though it shouldn't be. You know how teens get all riled up about the silliest things. Anyway, she didn't state it outright, but I think Emily really wants a flower because she doesn't want to look like a nobody. Do you think it would be wrong to buy her one? I wouldn't put my name on it, but at least when they deliver the flowers to the students in front of everyone she'll have one . . . Or do you think that's being dishonest? I wouldn't want to get her hopes up, thinking a boy likes her or something. We know what a disaster that can be. Or even worse, if everyone were to find out her grandma bought her a flower, well, Emily would probably never speak to me again . . . What do you think?"

Charlotte blew out a breath, releasing the tension with her words. She was only met by silence.

"Bob?"

Still no answer.

"Bob." She turned to her side, barely making out his profile in the dark. "Are you sleeping?"

For her answer, she heard a soft, shuddering snore. She didn't know whether to laugh or cry.

Instead, she curled her pillow tight under her chin.

"It's good to know that you're with me, Lord," she whispered into the night. "Although I wish you could put flesh on and hang out for a while."

She smiled to herself as she imagined Jesus hanging out with her during the day. Helping her wash the dishes, chatting over a cup of coffee, reminding her of items to add to her grocery list. He'd surely know what to do about Sam—about all the kids.

"God, I know you are always with me. Forgive me for forgetting that. I don't have to do this alone—ever. So, if you could, just remind me that you are real and you are available. No matter what I need."

"I'm not doing this alone," she mumbled into the night. "I'm not alone."

Chapter Eight

Sam shivered despite the five or six heavy blankets that covered him. They kept him warm enough, but they smelled like his grandparents' house. More than anything he wished he were in his old bed back in San Diego. More than anything he wished it was his mom's voice he was hearing through the wall.

Sam punched his pillow once. Then twice. It wasn't fair. He'd do anything to be with her again. *Why did this have to happen? Grandma talks about God, but I don't want to hear anything about a God who would do this.*

He listened close and tried to make out his grandma's words, drifting up through the floorboards. She was prattling on about something. She was talking soft enough that he couldn't make out what she was saying, but loud enough that he could clearly distinguish her tone. He knew she was probably talking about him, going on about how "disrespectful" he was.

Sam curled to his side and pulled the blankets tighter around him. *I don't care what they think—don't care what anyone thinks.*

He listened closer and realized he didn't hear his grandpa's voice. And that made him even madder. Grandpa treated the kids like they were just trouble—*a big bother*, as he would say. *He's probably sleeping. Figures.*

Grandma's voice eventually quieted, and soon the only sound was the creaking of the bare tree branches outside his window, shifting in the wind.

Sam sat up in his bed and turned on the lamp on the bedside dresser. He opened the top drawer and pulled out a blue book with a satiny cover. For as long as he could remember, the book had sat on the bookshelf in the living room of their various apartments all around San Diego. No matter where they'd moved, the bookshelf had been set up and the books placed in their familiar spots. After his mom's death, their baby books had been one of the things Grandma had made sure to pack and bring with them.

He'd found them just a few days ago when Grandma had asked him to go upstairs to put some things away in the attic. Even though it had sat in his drawer for a few days, he hadn't worked up the nerve to open it. Just looking at it made him think of his mom—and so much more than that.

Sam opened the first page, noticing the faint scent of dust.

Samuel Dillon Slater, February 11
7 pounds, 2 ounces — 21 inches long

He turned the page again and scanned the family tree. Grandpa Bob, Grandma Charlotte, Uncle Bill, Uncle Pete. For many years they'd just been names in this book. They'd been birthday cards with a ten-dollar bill tucked inside and sometimes rare phone calls and visits by people who seemed too nice to be real.

And now—they were real. Real, living, breathing people

in a place he couldn't wait to escape. Not because he hated his grandparents. He knew they were doing the best they could. It was just the other side of the family tree that drew him.

Sam ran his finger over his father's name—Kevin James Slater. More than any of the other kids, he remembered piggyback rides, water-balloon fights, and playing Nintendo together until late at night. The things he loved most about his dad were the things that most likely caused his parents to split. He saw now that his dad was just a big kid who seemed to be around day and night to play. It was his mom who had worked two jobs, had always been tired, and hadn't really had much time to relax.

Yet, whatever caused them to split all those years ago didn't mean it had to keep him and his father apart now. In fact, sometimes Sam wondered if his dad even knew about his mom's death. Surely if he did know, he'd come around—he'd want to be part of their lives again.

Sam turned to the next page, noticing the ink prints of his hands and feet. The footprints were slightly blurred as if he'd moved when they were trying to press his foot onto the page.

"Kickin' it even then," Sam mumbled to himself, forcing a slight smile. His throat felt tight and his chest seemed to be filled with cement, making it hard to breathe. He felt tears coming, but he was determined not to cry. Crying did no good. It wouldn't change things. All it would prove was that he was weak. And the fact was he wasn't weak—far from it. He was capable of taking care of himself, no matter what anyone else thought.

Yet he couldn't stop crying as he turned the next page. Tears trickled down his face and dropped from his chin as he noticed his mom's handwriting and how meticulously she'd kept notes about his first year—his feeding schedule, his first laugh, the first day he rolled over.

Sam said his first word today, "Dada."
Sam took his first steps. We were at the park.
I fed Sam carrots for the first time. He spit them out all over me.

Nothing went beyond her notice.
How come things had to change?

In the back of the book were photos of his mom and dad. From the pictures it looked like they were in a tiny studio apartment, but at least they looked happy. His dad especially. In almost every photo, Sam was on his dad's lap or on his dad's shoulders. In fact, the more Sam looked, the more he noticed there were very few photos of Sam and his mom—maybe because it was his mom who always had the camera in her hand.

Even now he could almost hear her voice in his head: *Smile, Sam. Smile big!* She was always taking photos, even after his dad left. Yet, he could tell that behind her own smile there was a lot of pain.

Sam dropped the baby book to the floor and curled to his side, remembering the day he realized his dad wasn't coming back. During the weeks before, there had been a lot of yelling—his mom at his dad, his dad at his mom, and especially his dad at Sam. Sam's room hadn't been clean enough; he'd forgotten to put his cereal bowl in the dishwasher; his sneakers had trailed dirt into the house.

And then, one day Sam returned home from school and there had been only silence. No one yelling at him. No one on the couch playing video games. His dad was just gone.

For a while after that Sam remembered being mad at his mom. She was the one who had started all the fights with his dad. Maybe if she'd done things differently, his father would have stayed. Or maybe if he'd been a better kid that would have made the difference.

"Yeah, maybe I caused too many problems," Sam mumbled to himself. His mind took him back to when he was seven. His dad had been sleeping, and Sam had been hungry. One of the only things in the fridge was a huge block of cheese in a brown box. He'd lugged it to the yellow countertop and then picked up a knife to cut off a piece. It had to be a big knife for such a big piece of cheese.

Emily had been taking a nap, just like he should have been doing, and Christopher had just been born.

The knife had been too big, too sharp and it had cut Sam's finger. It hurt, and he had cried. It was the first time he'd remembered his mom yelling so loudly. His mom had yelled at his dad for not watching Sam better. His dad had yelled because of the emergency room bill. And it wasn't long after that when his dad had left for good.

As the memory replayed, Sam felt seven again. He remembered the pain of the cut, but even worse was the pain of the yelling and his dad leaving. Then he thought of all that had happened since his mom's death—the move, the new school, the farm, his friends. Everyone seemed to be doing okay, everyone but him. Emily had a good friend in Ashley. She was doing okay in school. Christopher was doing even better than that. He actually seemed to like this place. He even liked his chores. He did everything Grandma and Grandpa asked, and even got super-excited about a dumb poem in a dorky school newspaper.

What's wrong with me? How come everyone else can handle everything better than me? I must have big problems if I can't get over little things like a birthday cake and my baby book . . .

Sam glanced at the small pile of presents he'd gotten. Things that people had bought because they thought he'd like them. But even those gifts hadn't made him happy. Nothing seemed to make him happy anymore. It was as if there was a black hole in his chest, and any bit of joy was sucked into it before he could pull it back.

He picked up the tickets for the snowmobile race on the top of the pile and fingered them. *Too bad I won't be around to go.* He pushed the image of his grandfather's disappointed face out of his mind.

In the glow of the lamplight he noticed the shimmer of the gold lettering of his name on the Bible. He reached over and picked it up, careful not to stretch too far and hurt his ribs.

The Bible looked nice with a black leather cover and gold along the edges, but it wasn't the Bible itself that Sam was interested in. He opened it up and noticed his mom's letter. The handwriting on the envelope was the same as in his baby book—big and loopy and girly—part girl and part woman.

He held the letter, taking in the feel of the yellowed paper, but he knew there was no way he could read it. Not yet. The baby book was hard enough to read, and it was just facts. His heart lifted, knowing that his mom had written home about him. He assumed that she must have said something good—otherwise Grandma never would have passed the letter on to him. But he couldn't help feeling a little guilty about that too. After all, his mom never would have run away or gone to California if she hadn't been pregnant with him.

Sam returned the letter to the front of the Bible and quickly closed it. He couldn't think about this anymore. He couldn't dwell on the past. The past wouldn't change, no matter how much he wished it would. Instead, Sam knew, he needed to think of the future.

Before turning off the light, Sam climbed out of bed and dropped his Bible into his tote bag at the end of his bed. He supposed it would be a good thing to take. One last thing to remember his grandparents by. One more thing to remember Mom by.

Chapter
Nine

The fumes from the engine caused Sam's stomach to flip, and an invisible weight pressed down on him as if the car's engine had been placed upon his shoulders. His grandpa stood next to him, leaning in under the hood and checking the new belt Uncle Pete had just installed. Like with everything else Pete did, Grandpa was eyeing things to make sure he'd done it right.

"Okay, looks good. Start 'er up." Grandpa called to Pete, who was sitting behind the steering wheel.

Sam stepped back and crossed his arms over his chest. He felt his shoulders shiver slightly but not because of the cold. It was warm inside the garage, almost as warm as inside the house. A bright floodlight poured light into his car's engine.

Sam had ridden the school bus home to find Pete hard at work under the hood. Seeing his uncle covered in grease, with his mind fixed on the task at hand, made Sam feel guilty. Pete thought he was helping, making it easier for Sam to get back and forth to work and school. Yet Sam knew his uncle had no idea that he was helping Sam escape. To leave this place. For good.

The engine roared to life, and Grandpa tilted his head to listen closer.

"Okay, shut 'er down. Sounds good."

Pete turned off the engine and Grandpa turned, pushing his ball cap off his forehead. "Sounds good. A new belt was just what was needed." He chuckled. "Looks like you'll be getting a new car after all—piece by piece."

"Thanks, Grandpa." Sam offered a slight smile. "Thanks, Uncle Pete," he called to his uncle, who was climbing out of the car.

"No problem. That's what family's for." Pete grabbed up his tools and began putting them away.

Great. Rub it in. Make me feel worse than I already do.

"So you heading to work today?" Pete glanced at his watch.

"No, I told Brad that I'll come in the rest of the week. I wasn't sure if my car would be running, although I shouldn't have doubted."

"I wish I would have had a job like that after school. Brad's a great guy." Pete fixed his eyes on Sam, and Sam was sure he could read the truth.

Sam quickly turned away. "Uh, yeah, Brad's great. I, uh, wouldn't do anything to mess things up there." Sam turned to the garage door. "I'm going to head inside. I have to help Emily with her homework."

Pete's eyes widened. "Really?"

"Yeah, algebra 2 is kicking her butt. I told her I'd help her out."

Pete chuckled. "Better you than me."

His grandfather followed him out. "I'll walk with you.

Maybe Grandma has something special waiting for us. I saw her mashing up bananas earlier. I bet banana bread is cooling on the kitchen counter as we speak."

Sure enough, scents of cinnamon and bananas and warm bread met Sam's nose as he entered the kitchen. Grandma was sitting on the couch, quizzing Christopher on his spelling words. Emily sat at the dining room table with her algebra books spread before her.

"Need help with that?"

Emily glanced up, surprised.

"Excuse me?"

"Do you need h-e-l-p?" Sam emphasized every letter in the word.

"Yeah, of course. Are you going to tell me to call a friend?" Emily turned her attention back to her work.

"I think your brother's trying to be nice," Grandpa said from the kitchen. He was slicing a large piece of banana bread, even though dinner was just an hour away.

"Sure," Emily tapped her pencil on the book. "It takes me ten minutes to work through one of these problems, but when I check my answer it's still not right."

"Let me see." Sam sank down in the seat next to her. His eyes scanned the problem. "Ah, I see that you've messed up the order of operations. You're supposed to solve the part in the brackets first. Then you'll be able to solve the rest."

Emily hit her forehead with a flat hand. "Duh, of course. I totally forgot. Thanks, Sam."

Sam nodded but he didn't move. Grandma paused from Christopher's spelling words and turned to him.

"Do you have any homework, Sam?" Grandma tucked her gray hair behind her ear.

"Uh, no. I turned in everything I need to." Sam's chest constricted as he thought about the essay due next Tuesday.

Still, Sam convinced himself he wasn't telling a lie. He had homework, but none he was planning to turn in. By the time it was due, he'd be long gone.

Emily paused from her homework and turned to him. "So, are you planning to buy a flower for anyone at school on Friday?"

Sam thought about a few girls who had turned his head lately, but he knew spending money on flowers was out of the question.

"No. You?"

"What's up with you, Sam?" Emily dropped her pencil on her paper. "First you want to help me with math. Then you sit here and talk to me about flowers."

"You're the one who brought up the flowers. I was just answering your question."

"Which doesn't make sense." Emily took one of the hair bands she had on her wrist and quickly put her blonde hair up into a ponytail. "Last week you were miserable to be around, and today you're acting like we're actually good friends or something."

Sam shrugged. "You don't have to answer my question if you don't want to, Emily."

Emily crossed her arms over her chest. "I thought about buying a flower for this guy at school—and I'm not going to say who—but it just seems weird to buy flowers for a guy, especially if they've given you no hint of liking you back."

"Do you think you'll get one?" Sam leaned his chin on his fist, resting his elbow on the table. As he looked at

Emily he realized how much she looked like their mom. He wondered if anyone noticed how much he looked like his dad. Even when he was little everyone always said it was obvious he was Kevin Slater's son.

"Okay, Christopher. That's enough spelling today. We'll go over them again tomorrow night, but it looks like you know them pretty well," he heard his grandmother say.

Christopher didn't have to be told twice, and he hurried to the kitchen to cut himself a slice of banana bread.

"Get a flower?" Emily's eyes brightened. "I'm not sure. It would be cool if I did, but what if someone I don't like gives me one? That would be awkward. Or what if it's someone that I do like . . ." Emily lowered her voice. "Grandma and Grandpa would have a fit. So that would be hard, you know?"

Sam nodded. He saw Emily looking over his shoulder. Then she leaned in close, whispering. "Grandma is totally spying on us. I think she's even more worried about the flower than I am."

As if realizing she'd been caught, Charlotte rose and looked at her watch. "Oh, look at the time. I told Hannah I'd run three eggs over. She wanted to bake a cake and didn't realize she was out. Do you mind if I stay for a cup of coffee too?" Sam watched as she approached him.

"Nope. I don't mind. Just going to watch a little TV until dinner."

"Yeah! *Wheel of Fortune!*" Christopher punched his fist into the air.

His grandmother left, and Sam rose, realizing he had some things he wanted to put in the trunk of his car without prying eyes.

"Wait." Emily grabbed his arm. "Do you want to hear my plan?"

"What do you mean?"

"Well . . . I was going to talk to Grandpa about putting on a surprise Valentine's Day dinner for Grandma."

"Sorry, I'm not going to be here."

"But I was hoping for your help."

Sam shook his head, and he lowered his gaze, glancing down at Emily and trying not to feel like a total jerk for what he was going to do to her and Christopher. "Sorry." His voice was firm. "I don't cook. I don't clean, and I don't do sappy, romantic holidays. And I wish you luck at trying to get Grandpa involved with your scheme."

"Thanks a lot, Mr. Hyde."

Sam ignored her remark. "Besides," he added, moving to the stairway leading to his room, "I'm staying the night at Paul's house, remember?"

Chapter Ten

Charlotte added a touch of red food coloring to the pancake batter and then attempted to make heart-shaped pancakes on the griddle. She chuckled, realizing they looked more like Mickey Mouse ears—but at least she tried.

"Wow, Grandma, you're going all out for Valentine's Day." Sam sniffed the air as he sauntered into the room. He glanced from the griddle to the stovetop. "You want me to make the syrup?"

"Sure."

Charlotte eyed her grandson suspiciously, wondering who'd replaced the moody teen. In the days since his birthday celebration Sam's attitude had improved. Maybe Bob's talk had done some good after all. But Charlotte still thought his cheerfulness seemed a little too forced.

Charlotte's first reaction was wondering just what Sam was up to. Maybe he was trying to butter her up before a bad progress report showed up in the mail. Or maybe he was going to try to talk her into getting one of those new video gaming systems. Then again, at least he was smiling.

I should just enjoy his attitude while I have the chance.

"Yes, syrup would be great. The corn syrup, brown and white sugar, and maple flavoring are above the stove." She pointed to the correct cupboard.

"Cool. I'll be right back," he hurriedly carried a white plastic garbage bag to the door.

Charlotte eyed it suspiciously. "What do you have in there?"

Sam glanced back and shrugged. "Just junk mostly. Old magazines. My old, torn-up sneakers. You know, stuff like that. I thought I'd clean up my room."

Charlotte flipped the pancake, hearing the sound of Emily humming as she headed to the shower upstairs. "Wow, Sam, I think you're the one who's going all out this morning. Did Grandpa give you another lecture I didn't hear about?"

"No, I thought I'd do it just because." He opened the door, letting in a gust of cold air. "Be right back, and I'll get started on that syrup."

Bob sauntered down the hall from the bedroom, rubbing a hand down his smoothly shaved face.

"Was that Sam? He's up and out early this morning."

"Actually, I'm not sure it was Sam. He cleaned his room *and* offered to help with breakfast. Maybe seventeen finally kicked in and he's decided to approach life with a little more maturity."

"Humph." Bob poured himself a cup of coffee. "We'll have to see about that."

Bob stepped behind Charlotte and offered her a peck on the cheek. "Happy Valentine's Day." Then he reached in his large overalls pocket and pulled out a card, placing it on the counter in front of her.

Charlotte felt her heartbeat quicken slightly. She turned and gave her husband a big hug. "Bob Stevenson, I think you have just made this my best Valentine's Day ever."

He chuckled in her ear. "But you haven't even opened it yet."

"It doesn't matter what it says. It's the fact that you went out and bought a card. That's enough." She wiped her hand on the kitchen towel and then opened the envelope.

Bob moved to the dining room table. "So maybe Emily was right. It's the thought that counts."

Charlotte opened the card, noticing a photograph of a pretty floral arrangement on the front under the words, "For my wife." There was a nice poem inside, but she had to admit that she was slightly disappointed that he'd only scribbled the words, "Love, Bob." There was no sweet note, no tickets to the movie theater in Harding, no invitation for dinner out. Charlotte noticed Bob's eyes on her and she smiled.

"Thank you, sweetheart. I love it," she said enthusiastically.

Sam hurried back inside, washed his hands, and then pulled out the ingredients he needed for syrup. "How much sugar?" Sam got out the measuring cups.

"Two cups brown, two cups white."

He measured them and put them in the pot.

"And corn syrup?"

"One-half cup, and one teaspoon of maple flavoring."

He whisked all the ingredients together on the stove top, and Charlotte tried to ignore the sticky mess he was creating. *What's important is that he's helping.*

Sam finished mixing those, then he looked at her expectantly.

"Now add four cups of water," she instructed. "Then bring it to a gentle boil."

She watched him as he worked, noticing how tall he'd gotten, how diligent he could be when he set his mind on something.

Thank you, Lord. I'll take this glimmer of hope. It's better than any roses and chocolate. She smiled at Sam as she watched him stir. *It's a great Valentine's gift. The best.*

THE SYRUP WAS HOT AND BUBBLY, and Charlotte carried some bacon and a large stack of steaming, red "heart" pancakes to the table. Four male faces looked at her with expectation, and as soon as she set the plate down, four forks scooped up the pancakes and plopped them on their plates.

"Where's Emily?" Pete asked as he poured a heaping ladle of syrup on his pancakes.

"Oh, you know. Up there trying to improve her looks." Sam smirked.

"Sam—" Charlotte frowned.

"I didn't mean anything bad. Just stating she's trying to get dressed up for Valentine's Day."

As if on cue, Emily jogged down the stairs. She was wearing a red, fuzzy sweater. The sweater fit a little big on Emily and it hung low over black leggings.

"You look lovely, Emily. That sweater looks great on you. And I like your hair that way."

Emily touched the back of her head where her hair had been twisted up and was held with a large clasp.

"Thanks, I saw in one of my magazines how to do this updo."

"Up*doo*?" Christopher chuckled with his fork halfway to his mouth. "You put *doo* in your hair? Emily, that's gross."

"Haha, very funny."

Emily scanned the table and wrinkled her nose.

"The peanut butter's on the counter, if that's what you're looking for." Charlotte pointed to the large jar.

"Thanks, Grandma." Emily grabbed it and sat down with the others, smearing a big peanut butter glob on her pancakes.

"At least she's eating some protein. It's just not natural for a girl not to eat meat," Bob stated, as if it was the first time they'd all heard it—which it wasn't.

"I get protein." Emily fixed her eyes on her grandfather and shook her head. "Remember, I was drinking that protein shake when I was watching you fix Sam's car?"

"Your car's running?" Christopher sat up straighter. "I call shotgun!"

"Yeah, we got it done, after school." Bob nodded. "The part worked great. It should keep it going for at least another week or two."

Sam frowned and glanced at the clock, and then turned to Emily. "You better hurry. I'm leaving in ten minutes."

"Ten minutes?" Emily's eyes grew wide. "There's no way. I still need to paint my nails and fix my makeup. I can't go to school like this."

Charlotte waited for a smart remark from Sam. Instead, he just rolled his eyes and shook his head in disgust.

"Then you'll have to ride the bus, because I can't be late for class, Emily." Sam's voice was firm. "You're always making me late."

"Who are you now? Mr. Responsible?"

"And is something wrong with that?" Sam's voice rose. "I have people on my case if I mess up—and apparently I have them on my case if I do something right!"

"Never mind, Emily." Charlotte patted Sam's arm. "I think

we can all see a difference in you. A good difference." She glanced to her granddaughter. "I can give you a ride. I have to pick up some things from Herko's for dinner tonight as it is. Sam, why don't you go ahead with Christopher?"

"Thanks, Grandma." Emily rose and hurried back upstairs. "I'll be down as quick as I can."

Bob stared in disbelief at Emily's plate, still mostly full of food. "She just thinks she eats," he grunted.

"Come on, pipsqueak, time to head for school." Sam took his dishes to the sink, grabbed his backpack, and then headed out the door.

"Pipsqueak?" Christopher slid on his jacket and then scratched his head. "I'm not a pipsqueak. Grandpa even said I'm growing taller, right Grandpa?"

"That's right, sport, I did."

Christopher's face brightened as he grabbed his backpack and headed out the door. "Hey, Sam, wait up."

Charlotte watched as Christopher ran out to Sam's car and climbed in. It looked cold outside, and the gray clouds on the horizons hinted of snow.

She turned to Bob and shook her head. "I'm not sure which has more duct tape—that car or that backpack."

"Both." He winked.

Keep them safe, Lord, she prayed as she watched Sam drive away. *Hold them in your hands. And, if you wouldn't mind, keep that old car running too. Because as far as I can tell, it will take a miracle.*

EMILY BLEW ON HER NAILS as Charlotte drove her little Ford to town. The heater was turned to the maximum, but it hadn't warmed up yet. It still blew lukewarm air on them.

"Good thing I didn't ride with Sam," Emily shook her hot-pink fingers in the air. "His heater works about as well as the rest of his car—which is almost not at all. I'm sure my fingers would have froze on the way there. Do you think nail polish freezes? I suppose it could, don't you think?"

"Hmm, I don't know." Charlotte glanced at Emily from the corner of her eye, noticing her granddaughter was prattling on. Emily always seemed to prattle when she was nervous. "I can't remember the last time I've painted my nails, and I don't really think I've thought about it freezing before."

"Oh, maybe we should do that, Grandma. After I get home from school I can paint your nails."

"Well, I don't know. I don't paint them because it's too much upkeep. My hands are in and out of the water all day, and the polish is usually chipped by the next day."

Charlotte looked to Emily and the disappointment on her face was evident.

"Then again, maybe it would be nice for Valentine's Day. Do you have any other colors—something that will look okay on an old lady?"

"Grandma, you're not *that* old. In California some of my friends' parents were as old as you. One of my friends' mom was fifty when she adopted her."

"Wow, that is ancient." Charlotte cocked an eyebrow. "Unfortunately, I'm just a wee bit older than that."

"Yeah, but you don't look it. The farm life has been good to you." Emily paused. "Grandma, did you live on a farm growing up?"

Charlotte straightened in her seat. "No, actually, I grew up right downtown in a very busy city."

"A city? Really?"

"Well, we thought it was a city, because we had everything

we needed close by, unlike others—like your grandpa, who lived way out in the middle of nowhere."

"Where was this city? Was it in Nebraska?"

"Yes, it was Bedford."

"Bedford?" the name shot from Emily's lips. "Bedford's not a city!"

"Oh, we thought it was. It was bigger then. And a lot of people worked in town. My father managed the movie theater in town—"

"Movie theater? When did we have one of those?"

"It was back in the early sixties, when I was in junior high and high school. For a while I was one of the most popular kids in school. Everyone asked if they could spend the night at my house on weekends because they knew that meant a free movie. Unfortunately, the theater burned down when I was a junior, and overnight my social life seemed to go up in smoke too."

Emily's jaw dropped open. "That's sad and so unfair." Satisfied her nails were dry, she tucked them into her jacket pockets. "That's strange. I always pictured you on the farm."

"Well, my grandparents on my mother's side lived on a farm. It's only about fifteen miles away. We'll have to drive you by the area sometime. Of course, they sold that about the same time I married your grandpa. It's a big business now, but last time I was out that direction the old homestead was still there. My grandparents fed cattle for market and raised corn and soybeans. I spent a lot of time out there growing up, especially in the summers, so I knew what I was getting into when I married your grandfather."

"What else did you do? In town, I mean. Life must have been pretty boring."

"Not really. In junior high my girlfriend and I used to

hang around the tennis courts at the high school. A lot of high school guys met there—and sometimes we even played tennis." Charlotte laughed. In her mind's eye she remembered the first time she saw Bob. He'd been goofing off with a friend, but she hardly gave him any mind. Bob had been too tall, too skinny, and too much of a show-off. Of course, by the time she'd met him again at the end of her junior year, all those issues had been resolved. He'd changed—or maybe she had.

"Is that all?"

"Well, sometimes we'd go to the soda fountain and get a root beer for a dime. Of course, that isn't around any more. Aunt Rosemary's Fabrics and Fun took over that spot about five years ago, but in between there was a beauty shop, a shoe store, and even a pet shop."

"Did you go to church? I mean the same one we go to now?"

"Yes. I'd go to social events and Sunday night youth group. My parents only attended church on Sundays. They saw it as part of their weekend routine, and the rest of the week was for work, or in my case, for school and my studies. So that was my 'rebellion,' having fun during the week by hanging out with the religious crowd." Charlotte glanced at her granddaughter. "Of course, something stuck, and I found a close relationship with God when I was mostly looking for fun."

Emily nodded, but she didn't comment. When they approached the school parking lot, Charlotte thought Emily would be eager to jump out, but as Charlotte stopped, Emily sat there for a minute.

"Did you have your own car?"

"Not my own, but my parents let me drive theirs. It was

a white and coral '55 Chevy Bel Air—which was basically a big boat with wheels. I got to drive it if I took my mother to work. She was a kindergarten teacher in the next town. My dad, of course, walked to work, but I can tell you it felt so cool driving that car to school. It would have been faster for me to walk, but it was worth it. In the early sixties not many kids had their own wheels."

Emily sat there for a minute, looking at Charlotte as if she was trying to picture her grandmother her own age. Finally, Emily picked up her purse and two schoolbooks from the seat beside her. "Thanks for the ride." Emily reached for the door handle. "And for the stories."

Even as she climbed out of the car Emily seemed hesitant, and Charlotte knew she must really be worked up inside if she'd rather listen to her grandmother tell stories about her life fifty years ago than go hang out with her friends.

"Sure. I enjoyed it too. See you after school. Have a great day." Charlotte watched as Emily sauntered into the school building with her school books pressed to her chest. She *did* want Emily to have a great day, but she also knew what Emily's nervousness stemmed from.

Charlotte circled the block, waiting for the bell to ring. Last night she hadn't been able to sleep well. At first she prayed for Emily to get a flower in that silly fundraiser. Then she considered asking Sam to buy one for his sister. Finally, she decided maybe she should just buy one for Emily and keep it anonymous. No one would have to know except her and the school secretary.

The bell rang and all the students disappeared inside. Charlotte parked the car and hurried inside, hoping that Emily's homeroom class didn't have a view of the front of the school.

Only a few kids walked the halls, and all of them seemed to be hurrying to their classes. Charlotte slipped inside the office, feeling nervous. Her stomach was as knotted as if she were robbing a bank.

"Hey, Margo." Charlotte waved to the receptionist, who was also a neighbor to Bob's sister Rosemary.

"Charlotte, good to see you." Margo Needleman pulled a heart-shaped lollipop from a coffee mug on her desk. "Happy Valentine's Day."

"Thanks." Charlotte took the lollipop and stuck it into her pocket. "Actually, that's why I'm here. I have a few questions about that flower fundraiser."

Margo chuckled, her strawberry blonde hair bouncing with her laughs. "Let me guess: you don't want Emily to come home today empty-handed. Or is it Sam? Boys, you know, sometimes make just as big a deal of it as the girls do."

"You were right the first time. It's Emily. Is it possible to buy a flower and not include the note?"

"You're going to buy a flower for Emily? That's so sweet! And, yes, you can buy the flower without the note, but if you'd like I can write the note for you."

She leaned over the high counter, closer to Charlotte. "After all, half the fun for the kids is trying to figure out who wrote it." Margo winked, her voice lowering to a whisper. "I'm becoming quite good at writing sloppy teen-boy hand-writing, if I say so myself. Maybe it's due to all these years of deciphering absence excuses supposedly written by their mothers. The smart ones get their girlfriends to write their excuses. But you aren't here to hear me go on, are you?"

Margo opened her desk drawer and pulled out a slip of paper. "Just write what you want here, and I'll do the rest."

Charlotte wrote something brief. "Dear Emily, you are a great girl. I just wanted you to know. With care, Anonymous."

She handed Margo the note with five dollars for the flower. Margo copied Charlotte's message onto a small form, wrote out a receipt, and then hurriedly handed it to Charlotte. Charlotte heard footsteps behind her.

"Well, thank you for all your help today. Have a good weekend." Charlotte's voice was singsong as she prepared to leave. She turned to find Nicole Evans, the pastor's daughter, there. Nicole gazed at Charlotte with curiosity, and then turned her attention back to the receptionist.

"Hey, Mrs. Needleman, Mr. M told me to come and get those notes from you to go with the flowers. We're sorting them all during first period."

"Notes, yes, of course." Margo quickly tucked Charlotte's note in the middle of the large stack. "They're right here, Nicole." She pulled a heart-shaped lollipop from the mug on her desk. "And Happy Valentine's Day."

Charlotte offered a small wave and then hurried out of the building, back out to the car. As she got inside, shivering in the cold, she tucked the receipt into her purse, hoping that Nicole hadn't seen it. After all, even worse than not receiving a flower from a guy was receiving a pity-rose from your grandmother and having everyone at school find out about it.

As Charlotte picked up a few groceries at Herko's, she wondered if it was okay to pray for things like flower fundraisers. And by the time she'd loaded the car and made it all the way home, she decided it was. After all, somewhere in the book of Matthew Jesus talked about God caring for the sparrows. Emily ate like a bird, it was true, but

Charlotte knew in her heavenly Father's eyes the young girl was far more important.

The mail was waiting on the table, and Charlotte put the groceries away and then glanced through the bills. The gas bill was up, as were the electric and phone, yet somehow by God's grace they made it through.

Charlotte opened the Visa bill last, not expecting there to be anything on it. Bob always believed in purchasing everything with cash, and he'd rather buy the things he needed from his friends downtown than save money by purchasing from some unknown person on the Internet.

She stopped short when she opened the bill and noticed a charge she didn't recognize. There was a set of initials followed by an Internet order number. Bob was out in the barn, and Pete was most likely with him. It was too cold to go out and ask them about a charge as small as thirty-nine dollars, so she put the bill with the rest and made a mental note to ask them about it when they were inside.

She threw a load of laundry into the washer and then a thought struck her. Pete had been ordering seeds. She could almost bet he'd ordered some online and had used her card to do so.

"Mystery solved," Charlotte mumbled. "Now, mystery number two awaits. What special treat can I make for Bob that won't make his sugar skyrocket?" It was a challenge, living with a man with diabetes, but Bob was worth it. Especially since this year he'd actually gotten her a card.

Yes, having the kids around was influencing *every* part of their lives.

Chapter Eleven

Emily tried not to look at the clock. She didn't want to seem desperate over the fact that the next ten minutes could change her life.

Will there be a flower for me?

The cheerleaders, including Nicole, had worn their uniforms to school today. The skirts were hardly long enough to be considered decent, but it was too late for the administration to comment.

As was tradition, the flowers were given out right before lunchtime. From what Emily had heard, it was quite a big production, with the cheerleaders coming in and calling out names of recipients, forcing them to stride to the front to receive their prizes.

Emily glanced two rows over and noticed Ashley's eyes meet hers. Ashley wore a smile, a natural smile, and Emily wished she could be so calm.

Remembering they were supposed to be reading the end of chapter 25, Emily turned her attention back to the page. The chapter was about Thomas Jefferson's role in westward expansion, but no matter how hard she tried to concentrate the words wouldn't sink in. She read the same paragraph five times to no avail.

"Hey, Emily, can I borrow a pencil?" Hunter, a new kid at school, leaned across the aisle.

"Uh, sure." Emily grabbed her backpack from under her desk and pulled it out. "It might need to be sharpened," she said as she handed it over.

"Thanks. It'll work." Hunter smiled. "Appreciate it. Tried writing with my fingernail and that didn't quite work."

Emily was trying to think of something clever to say back when the door opened and three of the cheerleaders walked into the room with Nicole in the lead. Nicole tossed her hair over her shoulder with one hand as she carried a large bouquet of flowers in the other. Emily glanced toward Hunter again and noticed his eyes were fixed on Nicole. She would have been annoyed by that, except for the fact that her heartbeat quickened with the thought that one of those flowers could be for her.

Just chill, she told herself. *It's no big deal.* Nicole let out a slow breath and came to a stop in the center of the room. *Oh, the drama*, Emily thought to herself.

"Christina . . ." Nicole glanced on her list. "Two flowers for you, with special notes."

Christina strode to the front of the room.

"Ooo, *two* flowers," a kid called from the back of the class. "Does that mean there will be a duel for your affection?"

Christina blushed, but only slightly, then she took the flowers and hurried back to her seat.

"Chad," Nicole called out.

"Madison."

"Dakota."

"Aiden."

One by one, her classmates went to the front. For some

of them, it was obvious who their flowers were from. But for others it was a mystery.

"Ashley."

Emily turned and glanced at her friend, who seemed genuinely surprised. Ashley hurried to the front, her face turning nearly as red as her hair.

"Now that's what I call a carrottop," Hunter said, chuckling to himself.

"Yeah, I don't think I've ever seen her face so red." Emily sat up straighter in her seat. "Ashley, who is it from?"

Ashley glanced at the note and then she pressed it to her chest, smiling. "I'm never going to tell. Ever!"

Emily smiled and then turned her attention back to the front, noticing Nicole only had a few flowers left.

"Emily." Nicole said, meeting her gaze. "You have a flower."

Emily knew every eye was on her as she strode to the front. She tried to act as casually as possible. She took the flower from Nicole's hand and then hurried back to the seat. She was halfway back when Nicole's voice split the air.

"Oh, Emily, wait. You have two flowers. You better come back."

Emily turned around and paused, sure Nicole was just trying to embarrass her. Still, her heartbeat quickened. *Two*.

Nicole held out the flower. "Seriously. I'm not joking. There's another one. It came in last minute."

Emily returned to the front.

"Another duel at sundown in the back parking lot." Someone called from the back.

Nicole laughed as she handed Emily the rose. "No, no need for a duel." She tilted her head and forced a smile.

"Unless your grandma likes to do that sort of thing. It must be a little sad, really, to get a *sympathy* rose."

The bell rang, and Emily hurried back to her seat just long enough to throw her book into her bag and head out the door.

"Hey, Emily, do you want your pencil back?" It was Hunter's voice that called to her through the crowd of kids talking about their flowers.

"No, keep it," she answered, hoping to hide the emotion in her voice.

Hot, angry heat filled Emily's chest. Why did Nicole have to do stuff like that? It made no sense. Nicole was prettier and more popular—and she would always be. Yet time and time again she insisted on making Emily's life miserable.

"Hey, wait up," Ashley said.

Emily's footsteps slowed just slightly.

"Wow, Emily. You got two flowers."

"Yeah, if you count the one from my grandmother." Emily spit out the last word.

"You don't know that. Does the paper say that? Let me see."

Emily pulled the notes closer to her chest. "No way. Do you think I want to embarrass myself any more?"

"Emily." Ashley tugged on Emily's arm harder. "Everyone knows how Nicole is. If anything, her comment made *her* look bad, not you. Now let me see."

Emily paused, and with a sigh she reluctantly handed over the notes.

"To Emily. I hope this flower brightens your day cause your smile always makes mine happier. Anonymous." Ashley handed it back. "Ah, very sweet!"

Then she read the second note. "Dear Emily, you are a great girl. I just wanted you to know. With care, Anonymous." Ashley gave that one back too. "Wow, those are really nice."

"The second one sounds like something my grand-mother would say. What teenager says 'with care'?"

Ashley chuckled, and somehow it made Emily laugh too. "Yeah, well, I *know* mine is from my mom. She used my middle name, and she's the only one who does that."

"Are you serious? No way."

"Yes, way." Ashley shrugged. "But I don't mind. I know she was just trying to make me feel better."

"Well, if I do find out this note is from my grandma, I'm going to kill her. I—"

"Emily?" It was Hunter's voice that cut off Emily's words. She turned and glanced up at him, hoping her face didn't register surprise.

"Uh, yeah."

"I was, uh, wondering if I could ride down to your farm sometime. It's pretty close to mine, and well, my mom says I need to do a better job at making friends."

Emily felt Ashley's elbow on her rib. "Yeah, of course. That'd be fun."

"Cool. Maybe sometime this weekend then?"

"Uh, yeah. Maybe so." She nodded enthusiastically as Hunter strolled away.

"*Ohmygosh!* Did you see that? I think he likes you."

Emily pressed her backpack to her chest. "No. I think he's doing what he said—just trying to make friends."

"Yeah, well, that doesn't matter. Whatever he's up to got someone totally jealous." Ashley's eyes were focused behind Emily. Emily turned and noticed Nicole's gaze upon them.

Then Emily turned back and hurried to her locker. Ashley walked beside her, matching her stride.

"Nicole could be totally making it up about my grandma— or it could be the truth." She sniffed the flowers in her hand. "But I suppose it doesn't really matter, right? I mean, what matters in the end is that I have two flowers—and personally, I don't see Nicole walking around with even one."

Chapter Twelve

Charlotte could hardly wait until the school bus rumbled down the road. When she saw it, she waited by the window and craned her neck, looking to see what Emily held in her hands.

She saw Emily exit from the bus with an extra hop in her step. Christopher hurried behind, pulling his stocking cap lower over his ears as he ran.

Charlotte saw a blur of red, and when Emily got closer she noticed she had not one rose but two.

"Two roses! Bob, do you see that? Emily has two roses."

"Goodness gracious, woman," he called from the living room, where he was reclining with a new western novel. "I think you're more excited about that than the day I gave you that silver bracelet and asked you to be my girl."

"Not quite," Charlotte chuckled. "But close. And just think . . ." She placed her hands on her hips. "I was worried she wasn't going to get one . . ."

At the same time, Charlotte's stomach knotted as she imagined her granddaughter getting involved with a boy. *I can't make up my mind, can I?* Charlotte bit her lip.

Toby scratched at the door, wanting to be let out.

Charlotte cracked the door open, and Toby darted toward the kids, barking with excitement as if seeing the kids was the best part of her day.

Emily opened the door and entered, beaming from ear to ear. Her cheeks were flushed, and Charlotte couldn't tell if it was from the cold air outside or the excitement of the day. Probably both.

"Hey, Christopher, Emily. How was your day?"

"Not great." Christopher shrugged. "One of the judges is sick and we won't find out who won the science fair until *next* week." He plunked his backpack onto one of the dining room chairs and swept Lightning into his arms.

"That's disappointing. More waiting . . ." Charlotte ruffled Christopher's hair, then she turned her attention to Emily.

"Look at those flowers! Wow, who are they from?" Charlotte asked, hoping that Nicole hadn't let Charlotte's little secret out of the bag.

Emily shrugged. "I have no idea. Neither card said." Her smile fell, and she eyed Charlotte. "Do you know, Grandma?" Emily walked to the kitchen window sill and filled the bud vase with water. She put the flowers into the vase and then returned it to the sill.

"Know? Me? How would I know?"

Emily eyed her grandmother for a moment. "I'm not sure. How *would* you know?"

Charlotte felt the hairs on the back of her neck stick up, and she was sure she'd been found out. She'd never been good at keeping secrets. In fact, Denise used to say that Charlotte's emotions were as easy to read as Bedford's weekly newspaper.

Then, just as Charlotte was about to confess to Emily

what she had done, Emily dropped her backpack on the table and hurried over to her grandfather. Emily leaned over and whispered something in Bob's ear, and Bob nodded. Then, as Charlotte eyed them, wondering what they were up to, they glanced in her direction.

"No keeping secrets!" Charlotte called into the living room.

"I can say the same to you," Bob shot back.

Charlotte folded her arms over her chest and feigned a frown, but she knew Bob was right. She had as much to hide as anyone around here.

"What secret?" Christopher asked as Lightning wiggled to get out of Christopher's grasp. Christopher released the cat, but as soon as she scurried away Christopher must have changed his mind. "Hey, Lightning, wait. Get back here, you silly thing!" Lightning raced upstairs and so did Christopher. Emily rose and moved to the stairs. "Okay, I'm going to go upstairs to, uh, clean my bedroom. Grandma, why don't you kick back and relax? Enjoy your needlework. Make yourself a cup of coffee."

Now Charlotte really knew something was up, but that didn't keep her from following Emily's orders. "Well, all right. I think I will," she mumbled to herself a minute after Emily had raced up the stairs. And for once it felt okay to ignore the list of chores that never seemed to get done— this time she had permission.

A smile still filled Emily's face thirty minutes later when she brought down a basket of dirty clothes. Charlotte was relaxing on the living room sofa, working on an embroidery project she'd put aside a few months ago and hadn't gotten back to. She knew she should be starting dinner, but secretly she hoped Bob would suggest going out to eat—

maybe even to Harding. *Perhaps that's what they were whispering about.* It wasn't something he typically did, but Bob had gotten her a card so anything could be expected.

Emily had just tossed a load of laundry into the washer and exited the laundry room when Pete entered, hurrying into the house, rubbing his hands together.

"Hey, Mom, you wouldn't happen to have any black shoe polish would you?" he called from the kitchen.

Charlotte glanced up and noticed that Pete wore nice dress slacks, a button-up shirt, and his dress shoes. He'd even put on a nice leather jacket that Bill and Anna had gotten for him a few Christmases ago.

"Yes, in the cupboard above the washing machine—top shelf." She couldn't help but appreciate how handsome Pete looked, or how much he reminded her of her own brother, Chet, when he was younger. Chet had always been a looker.

Pete hurried to the laundry room, and Charlotte could hear him rummaging around.

"Wow, Uncle Pete. I thought you were some stranger breaking into the house," Christopher called after him. He'd been sitting at the table the last half hour, working on his story for the school newspaper.

"Yeah, I've never seen you look so—clean." Emily giggled. Then she tapped her finger against her chin. "Actually, when you're all dressed up like that you kind of look like a movie star."

"Like a young Robert Redford," Charlotte commented.

"Who?" Emily frowned.

"Oh, just a movie star who was popular when I was young."

Pete entered the room again. "Mom, the shoe-polish can is empty."

"Sorry. I'll add that to my shopping list. But if you wipe your shoes with a damp rag it will help. How did they get so covered with mud?"

Pete opened his mouth to answer, but Emily gave a low whistle as she eyed her uncle again. Charlotte noticed Pete's cheeks turning pink.

Bob turned down the volume on the television and motioned to Pete to come in his direction. Pete shuffled into the living room and his face wore an apology as if he'd been caught playing with his dad's suit coat.

"Looks like you're off for a special night." Bob set the remote control on the side table next to his chair.

"Yeah." Pete shrugged. "I suppose."

"Well, I don't understand why you don't have a ring on that girl's finger. If you've got something that good, you don't want to lose it—again."

"It's not that easy, Pops. There's a lot of history. A lot of questions." Pete glanced at Charlotte and the kids, and instantly she felt guilty. She knew *they* were part of the questions Pete had.

How will he ever be able to start his own family when he's working so hard to take care of all of us?

"She's a lucky girl too," Charlotte added, hoping to encourage her son. "Did you buy her something special? A girl always loves surprises."

Pete's face grew pale. He stuck his hand into his jacket pocket and pulled out a small box of chocolates.

"That's it?" It was Christopher's voice that spouted out what they surely all wanted to say. "But I thought you liked her, Uncle Pete!"

"What do you mean? I do. Besides . . ." Pete shoved the box into his pocket. "She told me not to get her anything.

On the phone the other night, we talked about how commercial this day is. It's not even a real holiday, you know—"

"Uncle Pete, you're such a *man*," Emily interrupted. Then she glanced at the clock. "If you hurry now, I think you can make it. I heard a commercial on the country radio station that the flower store was staying open extra late tonight—you know, for poor saps like you who wait until the last minute."

"But I told you—" Pete's jaw cocked, as it always did when he was about to jump into an argument.

"I know what you said." Emily fiddled with a vase on the kitchen counter that held her two roses, refusing to make eye contact. "But I'm just telling you, even if a girl says she doesn't want anything, she really does. Right, Grandma?"

All eyes turned to Charlotte.

Charlotte reached over and patted her son's hand. "Actually, she's right. Girls—women—just say they don't want a gift to make sure the guy *really* likes her, because if he really likes her he will get her something nice anyway."

"Are you kidding?" Pete scratched his forehead.

"No wonder you're still a bachelor, Uncle Pete." Emily crossed her arms over her chest. "Don't you understand women at all?"

"No. I don't." He ran his hand over his hair, smoothing it again. "There are all these unwritten rules. How's a guy supposed to know? Man, there should be a manual on this or something." He glanced at his watch. "Okay, I really gotta run."

Bob nodded and smiled as if he enjoyed seeing his youngest son in such a state. Pete managed to handle the farm with ease, but maybe he wasn't beyond needing their help.

"Should you call after him and remind him he forgot to wipe his shoes?"

Charlotte waved a hand in the air. "Nah, he'll realize it—most likely when he's kicking them off." She shook her head and chuckled to herself. First, for the fact that it was one of the only times she'd ever seen Bob stick his nose into one of their kids' relationships. And second, mostly because Emily received *two* flowers and now saw herself as the resident love guru.

Charlotte had just risen to start dinner. She'd decided on shepherd's pie, one of Bob's favorites, when the phone rang.

"Hey, Grandma." It was Sam's voice. "I just finished up work for the day, and I was just making sure it was okay if I stayed at Paul's house."

"Paul. Yes, that's right. Did Paul talk to his parents about it?"

"Yup. They said it was fine with them. So it's okay with you?"

"Sure, but I didn't see you take anything extra—you know, your clothes. Your toothbrush."

"Yeah, I totally forgot—I, yeah." Sam sounded distracted. "I spaced out what day it was."

Charlotte moved the receiver to her other ear. "Well, do you want me to drive in and bring you some clothes? What about a sleeping bag?"

"Nah, we're guys, remember? We don't worry about stuff like that. It's only for one night. I can either sleep in my clothes or borrow something. And I'm sure he has a sleeping bag I can use."

"Fine. I suppose one night won't hurt." Charlotte chuckled, remembering the numerous times she'd packed Bill's and Pete's items for a sleepover—or even for summer camp—only to discover them still neatly packed just as she'd left them.

"Cool. Good-bye."

"Sam," Charlotte interrupted. "Do you know what time you'll be home?"

"No. I don't know. Paul might have stuff planned. I'm not really sure."

"Okay, well, don't stay out too late. Remember that your grandpa's taking you to the races on Sunday."

"Yeah, okay." Sam's voice sounded muffled as if he had his hand over the receiver.

"Also, make sure you call me before heading home tomorrow. Your car's been acting up, and I don't want you to break down somewhere."

"Okay, sure. Talk to you later," Sam said hurriedly, and she thought she heard the sound of a car honking.

"Sam, where are you?" Charlotte asked. "What's all that noise?"

"Oh, nothing." Sam laughed loudly in her ear. "Paul just has the TV on a little loud. We're finishing up a movie, and then we're gonna play video games. You know, stuff like that. I'll call you tomorrow."

"All right. Have a nice ni—" The dial tone interrupted Charlotte's words.

"That Sam?" Bob asked, cutting himself a piece of sugar-free pie that Charlotte had made from the last of the summer berries in the freezer. She thought about scolding Bob—telling him not to ruin his appetite for dinner, but then she realized she hadn't even started it yet.

"Yes, and I'm hoping things are turning around for him. Yesterday he cleaned his room without being asked, and tonight he's sleeping over at Paul's house."

"Did he get his chores done before he left?" Bob asked.

Charlotte nodded. "I'm sure he did this morning. I saw him doing something out there. He carried out some trash from his room and then headed into the barn."

"We'll check, Grandma." Emily grabbed her jacket off the hook. Then she swept her arm before her.

"Farm boy, wish to join me in the barn?" Emily grinned at Christopher like the princess in *The Princess Bride*. "We have much work to do before supper."

"As you wish," Christopher said as he bundled up and followed Emily outside to feed the animals. They seemed almost eager to do their afternoon chores—without being told. Charlotte thought she should pinch herself. They usually never did their chores without being reminded at least once.

"At least Sam is connecting with his friends." Charlotte cut a piece of pie for herself. "In fact, it's a good night, Bob. At least for this moment it feels like we're turning a corner." She let out a sigh. "It seems that good things are coming around the bend."

Chapter Thirteen

Emily and Christopher finished their chores in record time, whispering between themselves as they unloaded the dishwasher. Watching them, Charlotte had a feeling something fishy was going on. And then, like a stone falling in the pit of her stomach, she wondered if she'd missed something important. Something she should have clued into sooner.

Earlier that day she'd noticed Valentine's Day gift baskets for kids and teens at the grocery store. At the time they seemed silly and commercial, but what if her grandkids were expecting something like that from her? Had Valentine's Day been a special day in the Slater household? Did Denise turn it into an event? Were Emily and Christopher eagerly expecting something—a nice dinner? Gifts? A special dessert? She had gotten a box of sugar-free chocolates for Bob and had left them on his nightstand with a card. He'd obviously found them because the last time she was in the room a third of the chocolates were gone.

Charlotte's mind scurried to think of what she could come up with. *If I hurry I can whip up some sugar cookies for the kids to decorate while dinner's cooking. I think there is some ice cream too* . . . Charlotte's mind worked on a plan. She also nixed the idea of shepherd pie. That was too everyday. Too ordinary.

"All done, Grandma," Christopher said as he hung the dishtowel on the rack. Then, casting a smile her direction, Emily and Christopher scurried up the stairs. Charlotte put down her embroidery.

"Good job," she called to them, pleased with herself for enjoying the time to relax. "The kitchen looks nice."

She glanced at Bob as she got up from the couch. "Guess I should get started on dinner. I think the kids are expecting me to make them something special."

Bob nodded and smiled at her, and then glanced at his watch. "Well, it is a special day." His tone was lighthearted, and Charlotte noticed a twinkle in his eyes.

Bob must be expecting something too. Thoughts ping-ponged around her mind as she tried to think what she could do. In the past they did very little to celebrate this holiday.

Charlotte was about to nix her plans for making a special meal and suggest they all go to dinner in Harding when Bob stood and looked out the window.

"Would you look at that, Char? Here comes Hannah. Did you know she was coming over today?" He glanced at her awkwardly and then stuck his hands in his pockets.

Charlotte followed Bob's gaze, and sure enough, she spotted Hannah's car turning onto their driveway.

"What's she doing here? I thought she said she was going out tonight—on a Valentine's Day date."

"Dunno. But you better get the door for her." Bob attempted to hide a grin. "Maybe she's making a special delivery."

Charlotte had just gotten to the side door when Hannah

burst inside with two large bags in her hands. "Whoa, the wind's really picking up out there! That storm's blowing in."

The bags in her hand read Mel's Place, and Charlotte didn't have to open them to understand that her dinner had just been delivered. And that her family didn't expect something special—but rather had planned it. Warmth filled her chest, mixed with disbelief. And for the briefest moment she understood how those Publishers Clearing House winners must feel. She wondered if Hannah had been behind it all.

"Hannah. What in the world are you doing? I thought you were going out tonight. Are you and Frank joining us? That would be a special treat." Charlotte noticed that Hannah was dressed up. Her normally faded jeans and favorite goose sweatshirt had been replaced by a red belted jumper and black faux-fur jacket.

"Joining you? Oh no, we wouldn't want to intrude on such a special evening." She put the bags on the counter. "We're actually heading over to my sister-in-law's house. It's their thirtieth anniversary, and their kids came in from out of town. I'm just here dropping off the first of your surprises."

Bob glanced between the two women as if he was unsure of what he should do next. He moved toward the stairs and looked up as if seeking help from above.

"Surprises? There's more?" Charlotte planted her hands on her hips. "Yes, I have to admit I'm completely surprised."

Hannah offered Charlotte a quick hug. "Okay, I've got to go. I don't want to be late. Have fun! And happy Valentine's Day."

After seeing Hannah out, Charlotte moved to the first bag. The aroma caused her stomach to rumble. "Not so fast, Grandma! Grandpa, don't let her look!"

Emily hurried down the stairs, her high-heeled shoes clomping on each step. She was wearing the black skirt and polka-dotted shirt she saved for special occasions, and Charlotte realized that the kids were in on this too. Actually, from Bob's uneasiness, she would bet that they were the ones who'd planned it—dragging their grandpa along.

Christopher followed Emily down. He was wearing the same pants he'd worn to school but had put on a clean shirt and had combed his hair. Charlotte grinned. She didn't have the heart to tell him that he'd buttoned the shirt one button off. It warmed her heart to see they were all part of the surprise.

"What in the world is going on?" Charlotte ran her hand through her short hair, suddenly feeling underdressed.

Emily placed her hands on Charlotte's shoulders and turned her in the direction of her bedroom. "You're gonna find out soon enough, Grandma. Now, I suggest you head to your bedroom and put on something nice. Maybe that blue dress you like to wear to church? Grandpa and I are going to get everything ready—right, Grandpa?"

"Uh, yes, of course we are." Bob's words sounded confident, but the look on his face showed just the opposite.

Charlotte went to her room feeling a little giddy. She grabbed her favorite dress—grateful that it was clean and pressed—and hurried into the bathroom to freshen up. She found herself humming as she dressed and then ran a brush through her hair.

Just as she was exiting the bathroom, she found Bob in their room, buttoning up a clean shirt.

Similar to Christopher, Bob had put on a dress shirt but had kept on the same blue jeans he'd been wearing all day. *Like grandfather like grandson.*

Charlotte offered her husband a quick hug. "Bob, what *are* you up to?"

"Oh, about six foot one."

She poked his ribs. "Seriously . . ."

"You'll see. It's something we've been plannin'—at Emily's insistence, of course. And I'm pretty proud we were able to pull this off. You didn't suspect a thing." He stepped closer and took her face in his hands. "You look beautiful, Charlotte, as pretty as the day we met. You didn't have to change your outfit."

"Not change? Getting dolled up is half the fun." She stretched up on her tiptoes and offered him a quick kiss. "Can you give me five more minutes?"

"Make that ten. We have to set the table and such."

"Okay, ten it is."

Bob hurried to the kitchen, and Charlotte closed the door and leaned against it. True, some women were dining at fancy restaurants, and others might be receiving jewelry in velvet boxes, but to her *this* was romantic. Her guy in a dress shirt, making dinner plans so she didn't have to cook. It had to be one of the most romantic things ever.

Charlotte let out a contented sigh as she dabbed her wrists with her favorite perfume.

This will be a Valentine's Day to remember.

CHARLOTTE RE-ENTERED the living room in her blue dress and black heels, and stopped short. Bob was standing at the dining room table, poised and smiling as if he'd just stepped out of a Big and Tall catalog.

"Oh, Grandpa, you almost forgot." Emily grabbed the single white rose from the kitchen counter, hurried to the dining room, and thrust it into his hand.

"Ma'am." Christopher approached with a towel draped over his arm. "May I get your chair for you?" He pulled out the dining room chair.

"Why thank you. What a delightful young man." Charlotte winked at Christopher.

Emily approached with a very grown-up look on her face. "Here is this evening's menu, ma'am." Emily had handwritten the menus in her best script. Charlotte read over the menu:

Today's Special: Dinner of Love
French Onion Soup
Tomato Basil Salad
Parmesan-Crusted Chicken
Garlic Potatoes
Roasted Carrots
Chocolate Heart Tarts with Raspberries

Under this was more script, written in Christopher's messy cursive. "Roses are red, violets are blue. Sugar is sweet, and so are you."

"Why, all this sounds wonderful. I can't wait to start." Charlotte patted her belly. "I love French onion soup."

"Me too. I'm starving." Bob pulled a lighter from his pocket and lit the two large rectangular candles in the middle of the table. It took three times to get the new wicks to stay lit, but Charlotte didn't mind waiting. She actually thought his fumbling around—unsure of what to do—added to the romance. When the candles finally stayed lit, Christopher shut off the overhead lights.

Charlotte peered closer, recognizing those candles. They were from her hutch and had been a gift from Pete one year for her birthday. Those candles had sat there for three years at least, and had never been used—just like the crystal candleholders that still remained safe and protected. She wondered why she always put off using her nice things—as if there was something better in the future she needed to save them for. Shouldn't every day with her family be a special occasion?

Charlotte watched Emily in the kitchen. She was pouring soup from a Styrofoam container into two bowls. Emily tested the temperature with her finger, frowned and then put the soup into the microwave for a minute.

Charlotte unfolded the cloth napkin that someone had dug out of the bottom drawer of the hutch and placed it on her lap. She had no doubt this whole thing was Emily's idea, and she was grateful.

For years she and Bob had gotten into a predictable rut, where neither gave much thought to celebrating special events or even being romantic. Life had become focused on taking care of the farm, their children—and now their grandchildren—and each other.

Emily served their soup, and Christopher brought over two glasses of ice water with lemon wedges.

Bob and Charlotte bowed their heads in unison as Bob prayed, "Lord we thank you for this food, this family, and the love we share." Charlotte wiped away a tear as she picked up her spoon.

The soup was a bit hot, and Charlotte blew on it. When it was finally cool enough, she took a spoonful and made a mental note to ask Melody for the recipe. There was an ingredient that added an extra zing.

"This is delicious," Charlotte said.

She glanced up and noticed Bob watching her. He glanced to Emily, as if looking for a cue of what to do next.

"Talk about something romantic," Emily cued in a loud whisper.

"You know, Charlotte, this reminds me of our first date." He leaned forward and rested his arms on the table.

"Our first date?" Charlotte chuckled. "Bob Stevenson, you must be thinking of some other girl, because our first date was going to eat pizza and then driving around."

"Driving around? Where did you drive?" Christopher asked.

"Shhh." Emily jabbed her brother with her elbow. "We're not supposed to interrupt. We're supposed to be invisible, remember?" Yet even though Emily scolded her brother, Charlotte noticed Emily leaning forward on the kitchen counter as if wanting to know the answer to the question.

"Well, Mr. Waiter," Charlotte said, addressing her grandson. "We drove all over the countryside."

"Yeah, we must have used up a whole tank of gas," Bob mumbled.

Charlotte glanced at Bob. "Remember, you drove me out here to your parents' farm. That's the first time I'd ever taken a real good look at Heather Creek Farm. Then we drove to my grandparents' farm next. Personally, I was glad we drove so much."

"Why?" Bob asked. He looked puzzled.

"Because my mother always told me that the day I parked with a boy was the last date I'd ever go on, and I was smitten—I definitely didn't want it to be our last date."

"Grandpa?" It was Emily who interrupted this time, but Charlotte didn't mind. "Why does this dinner remind you of your first date?"

Her two grandchildren seemed transfixed with seeing their grandparents sharing a romantic dinner together. Maybe it was because it was something new and different. Seeing the interest and joy on their young faces reminded Charlotte that they hadn't grown up with a mom *and* a dad. Whatever they saw concerning romance they'd gotten from TV. No wonder they were so interested in being part of this dinner.

Bob cleared his throat. "Well, it reminds me of our first date because your grandma's just so pretty. As pretty today as she was back then."

"Bob Stevenson, that's the second time you've told me that tonight." Charlotte could feel the heat rising to her cheeks. Bob wasn't one to give compliments often, but when he did she gladly accepted them.

"Well, dear, that's because it's true."

"Salad's next," Christopher interrupted, bringing out the next course. Charlotte nodded as she took a bite. "Yes, I remember this salad dressing recipe. I think I learned to make it in home ec."

"Me too," Bob said. "Although mine turned out so bad even the dog wouldn't eat it. In fact, I believe the garbage disposal spit it out too." He laughed.

"No way." Emily's face brightened. "Grandpa took home economics? I had no idea you know how to cook, Grandpa."

"I didn't then, and I still don't. But that's where all the girls were. I wasn't stupid, you know."

"So you met in home ec?" Christopher's eyes grew wide.

"I was a senior. Your grandma was a sophomore. Of course, she didn't give me the time of day back then . . ."

They talked and laughed some more, and by the time the main course was served, Christopher and Emily had pulled up two chairs to the table and had joined in. It was a good thing too, because Melody had outdone herself with the portions. Charlotte glanced around at the smiling faces, and she could only think of one thing missing—Sam.

"You know, I can't remember the last time we ate dinner by candlelight. We should do this more often. Maybe when we're all here."

Though she was disappointed that Sam hadn't been a part

of this night, Charlotte was happy that he was with Paul—spending some much-needed time with his buddies. She hoped Sam would get more settled with Jake and Paul, and they'd become better friends. Even now, Charlotte resisted the urge to call Sam and see how everything was going. Sam was nearly an adult now—seventeen. And with good choices like this would come ever greater freedom in the future.

Charlotte knew she'd just have to get used to it.

SAM SAT IN THE FOLDING CHAIR next to Paul's computer, staring at the screen but not really seeing it.

"Have you seen the one where the guy totally biffs it off the handrail? Oh, man, you gotta see this."

Paul opened the YouTube video, and Sam tried to focus on the shaky video of a kid trying to jump to the top of a handrail so he could ride down it. Six inches too low, the kid's knees hit the rail and he flipped, flying through the air like a rag doll before finally crumbling at the bottom of the step. Sam had seen the same type of thing a dozen times before in real life. Still he tried to react, for Paul's sake.

"Man, that musta hurt." Sam cringed, pretending he was as into the videos as Paul was. The truth was, his mind was fixed on the snow outside the window. It fell white and heavy.

"Hey man, can you look up the weather report?" Sam flipped his hair across his forehead. "You know, just to see what it's doing tomorrow . . ."

"Yeah, okay . . ." Paul clicked to another skateboarding video of a kid trying to jump an empty, plastic trash can on his skateboard. The kid didn't get high enough, and he fell into the trash can and then bounced off, landing on his shoulder. More laughter burst from Paul's mouth. "Man, what was he thinking?"

Sam took another drink of his soda and ignored the tension tightening around his chest, even though he tried to act as if today was just like any other day. On the inside it felt as if someone was wrapping bailing wire around him, pulling tight and tying it down.

Paul glanced over at Sam, as if suddenly remembering he'd asked about the weather. "Why do you need to know the weather?"

Sam shrugged. "Oh, I was just thinking maybe we could snowboard or something tomorrow. Just wanted to make sure the weather would be good."

"Yeah, we probably could mess around on the back hill. Paul chuckled and punched Sam's arm. "I'll check it out."

Paul typed in the address for the weather Web site, and Sam leaned forward. A smile curled his lips as he noted it would be clearing up after breakfast.

Long enough to get me down the road . . .

"So you want some chips or something? My mom said we had to fend for ourselves until Jake got here with the pizza."

"Sure, got any sour cream and onion?" Sam rose, excitement causing his heart to pound harder.

One more night . . . then so long, Nebraska.

"Hey, is Jake bringing over his game controllers too?" Sam took the steps from the basement to the kitchen two at a time.

"I told him to."

The kitchen was modern and fancy—unlike his grandma's kitchen back home. At first when he'd moved to Grandma's house, Sam had thought of that kitchen as foreign and ancient. Now it was hard to believe there'd been a time when he hadn't felt comfortable there. He opened Paul's fridge and noticed there were just a few jars and some containers of leftovers. His stomach growled, and he wished he could have a piece of his grandma's homemade bread with strawberry jam or maybe a nice thick meatloaf sandwich. *One last time.*

There was a pounding on the kitchen door, and Sam turned to see Jake's face pressed against the glass. Paul hurried over and opened the door. A stream of cold air flooded into the house, and with the arctic air came a flurry of snowflakes.

"Hurry, man, get in here and shut the door. If the floor gets all messed up we're gonna have to be the ones to clean it up."

Jake stepped in and stretched out the two pizza boxes in his hands, as if he were offering the pizza as a peace offering.

"Dude, chill. How was I supposed to open the door with my hands full? If you want a piece of the pie . . . you better welcome the guy."

Sam moaned. "Please tell me you didn't just say that." Still he couldn't help but laugh at the dorky look on Jake's face.

Jake set the half-cold pizza on the counter, and Sam grabbed a piece, taking a big bite. Jake emptied his pockets that held one game controller and two video games he'd been wanting to play for a while.

"Dude, we're going to be up all night at this rate." Sam smiled, realizing he actually enjoyed being around these guys. And as he took another slice of pizza he made the decision just to enjoy the night. Not to think about tomorrow. Not to think of his car that had a horrible heater. Or the snowy, icy roads heading out of town.

Chapter Fourteen

"Hey, Grandma, listen to this."

Charlotte had barely stepped into the kitchen when Christopher's words interrupted her thoughts—or rather lack of thoughts. She'd been headed to the coffeemaker, and she could tell from the eager look on Christopher's face that he wasn't going to wait for her to have a first cup before he read the paper he was waving in his hand.

"What's that, Chris?"

The ringing of the telephone interrupted her words. Charlotte glanced at the clock. It was before 8:00 AM, and there were very few people who called at this hour. She immediately thought of Sam. Was he already ready to come home? Was it a sign that the night hadn't turned out so well after all?

"Hello?" Charlotte answered.

"Mom, it's me, Anna."

Charlotte released the breath she'd been holding. "Anna, hi. How are you? How are Bill—and the girls?"

"We're all great—just great. But I was listening to my voice mail, and I just heard the message you left last weekend about Sam's birthday. I don't know how I missed it unless Bill listened to it and saved it without telling me."

"Oh, I understand." Charlotte rubbed the sleep out of her eyes, and then cradled the phone between her shoulder and ear as she turned her attention to the coffeemaker.

"We had a nice time. I made Sam's favorite cake." Charlotte stopped short of mentioning that Sam hadn't eaten a piece, or that he hadn't seemed impressed with his presents. When it came to Anna, Charlotte always felt as if she couldn't let her weaknesses show.

"Yes, well, I still feel horrible, and I did get Sam a little something. Will you be around this afternoon for me to swing by?"

"Actually, Sam's staying at a friend's house. He probably won't be in until later. Why don't you guys just head over for dinner?"

As soon as the words were out of her mouth Charlotte wished she could take them back. Anna was an excellent gourmet cook, which meant that now Charlotte would need to make a trip to town because the spaghetti sauce she was planning on whipping up just wouldn't do. She knew she shouldn't let her daughter-in-law intimidate her like this, but Charlotte wanted Bill's family to feel welcome in his childhood home. And if it took fancy-schmancy food to accomplish that, then so be it.

A little extra effort in order to have some family time shouldn't be a bother. This was what life was about—these people God had brought into her life. "Can you come?" Charlotte asked again.

"Well, we don't have plans. So yes, we would love to come for dinner." Anna's voice had an uncharacteristic lightness to it that made Charlotte glad she had asked. "It's been ages. Is six o'clock okay? Why don't I bring a salad?"

"Sounds great. We'll see you at six. And I'm sure Sam will be thrilled that you were thinking of him."

"Yes, well, it's just a little something that Bill helped me pick out. I'm not too familiar with teen boys—"

Charlotte heard one of her granddaughters call to Anna. "Looks like Jennifer needs my help with the computer printer. It's been acting up lately. I better go. See you tonight."

Charlotte hung up the phone and turned to see Christopher standing there, waiting for her attention.

"Can I read it to you now?" he asked.

More than anything Charlotte wanted to start her coffee, pour a cup, and then curl onto the couch and read her Bible. Yet Christopher looked so adorable in his pajamas and ruffled hair that she couldn't say no.

"Sure, what is it?"

"My story. For the school paper, remember?"

"Oh, yes." Charlotte leaned against the counter. "How could I forget? Is it about life on the farm?"

Christopher nodded and then cleared his throat, lifting the paper so he could read it better. "Maybe people think that winter on a farm is boring. Sometimes they are right, but there is exciting stuff going on too. Since this is my first winter on a farm I've learned a few things." Christopher paused and glanced up at Charlotte. "I don't have the whole thing written. This is just the beginning."

Charlotte retrieved the coffee canister from the cupboard and opened it, breathing in the aroma. "Okay, go ahead. Sounds good so far."

Christopher cleared his throat and then continued. "First, my grandpa says that on a farm it's important to work smarter, not harder," Christopher read. "That's why he taught me how to melt snow in big barrels inside the barn.

Grandpa says this does as good a job as a long hose, a well, and an electric pump.

"The first time Grandpa told me to do this he said, 'Fill 'em up, cover them with clear plastic, and wait a day.' Grandpa said that even on a cold day it stays about 50 degrees in the barn." Christopher glanced up.

Charlotte offered him a smile as he continued.

"The next day I went in and the snow had melted! I added more snow to the top and waited until the next day. I did that a few more times, and soon I had fifty gallons of rainwater in a barrel. The horses and cows don't seem to mind that they're drinking snowflakes." Christopher giggled. "That's just the first part—"

"Grandma!" Emily's voice interrupted. Charlotte could tell she was calling down from the top of the stairs.

"Yes, Emily?" Charlotte called back, too tired to move from her spot.

"Can Ashley stay over tonight? I promise I'll do my chores. Ashley will help too."

Charlotte couldn't think of a good enough excuse not to agree. "Yes, fine. But shouldn't you wait a little longer to call her? You don't want to wake up the whole household with a ringing phone, do you?"

"Don't worry, they're up!" Emily called.

Charlotte cocked an eyebrow as she listened to the scampering of Emily's feet across the floor as she ran to the upstairs extension. Then she turned her attention back to Christopher. "Your story is good. That is so creative, drinking snowflakes. You know . . . that would be a good title for the story."

"Yeah." Christopher nodded. "So, do you think it would win the prize?"

Charlotte bit her lip. She doubted that information about

melting snow would win a story contest, yet she wondered how she could help Christopher without hurting his feelings. "Well, Christopher, to me it sounds a little more like a report than a story." Charlotte tried to be gentle.

"What do you mean?" Christopher's eyebrows folded into a frown.

"I mean you're just telling about what Grandpa taught you. It's good, but there's no *scene*. Maybe you should try to write it so that you take us on an adventure with you—so we, the readers—can experience the event through your words."

"So a scene is something you can *see*?" Christopher nodded, jotting down notes.

Charlotte rinsed out her glass coffee carafe then filled it with clean water and poured it into the back of the coffeemaker. Then she approached Christopher and placed a hand on his shoulder.

"More than that, it needs a little mystery—something that makes us curious, so that we'll want to keep reading until the end."

"But it's sort of like a mystery, isn't it? I said that farming is exciting." Disappointment filled Christopher's face. His eyes widened, and his lips turned down in a slight frown. "I'm writing nonfiction, right, which means it has to be true . . ."

"Oh, there're all types of true things that are exciting. Like the mystery of the missing vegetables last fall. Or the tornado that hit the farm."

"Oh, I get it. Those were true stories that were *really* exciting."

"All stories need something like that to grab the reader's attention. Also, they need *conflict*, which is a fancy word for 'problem.'"

"The tornado was a conflict." Christopher scratched his chin.

Charlotte chuckled. "You can say that again."

"And what else? What else does a story need?"

"Well, characters who we want to get to know. And a good ending. Maybe you can think about some of the really exciting things that have happened lately."

"Like winning the pie contest?"

"Sure." Charlotte pointed her finger into the air. "Like that. And you're right when you told us life on the farm is exciting, but you need to show us. Take us on one of those adventures you always seem to be a part of."

Christopher shrugged. "I guess . . ." He scratched his head. "But there hasn't been anything exciting lately around here . . ."

What exciting thing hasn't *happened?* Charlotte shook her head. At least things were calming down, and last night was proof. She smiled at the memory.

SAM STRAINED HIS EYES as he peered out onto the blinding snow. Although it was before noon, the snow made it seem like it was much later. *So much for the stupid weather report. Is this what they call clear?*

His hands gripped the steering wheel as he focused on keeping his little car on the road.

The weather was far worse than he imagined it would be, and his heart pounded in his chest every time the strong wind pushed against the vehicle. He wished he had a car made for the weather—something like his grandfather's truck. There was nothing he could do about that now.

Sam was on his way to find his father, Kevin Slater. He was committed, and there was no turning back.

From the map he'd printed out from the Internet the drive

to Golden, Colorado, had seemed simple. Get on the interstate, head west, take a few turns, and he would be there.

In fact, the whole project to find his dad had seemed to fall into place. Once Sam had found his dad's name on the Internet and had realized that he was only an eight-hour drive away, it seemed obvious that he *had* to go. He couldn't rest knowing his dad was out there—so close.

Yet for a while Sam doubted he could pull it off, especially with his car acting up, threatening to ruin all his plans. Then when his Uncle Pete got the right part and fixed the car earlier in the week, everything again seemed like it would be okay. Even his grandma's willingness to let him stay the night at Paul's house had worked into his plan. It had given Sam time to leave unnoticed. It had allowed him a head start before anyone could come looking for him—not that they could find him anyway. Sam was certain that when his grandparents discovered he was missing that they'd check San Diego first. He was the only one who knew his dad was in Golden.

Before sunrise I can be there. I'll be able to see my dad after all this time.

Sam glanced at his gas gauge and realized it was getting close to empty. He saw a sign for a small town up ahead, and took the next exit.

The road heading into town wasn't as plowed as the highway. His car started sliding in the snow, drifting back and forth, forcing Sam to concentrate to stay on the road—not that he could see his lane. He had to guess. The only hint he wasn't driving into the ditch was the narrow tracks left by the vehicles that had gone before him.

"C'mon. Stay on the road." He tapped his thumbs on the

steering wheel, trying to spend some of the anxiety building in his chest.

Slowly, carefully, he drove his car into the gas station. He sighed deeply, feeling the tension ease from his body. He climbed out of the car, and the cold air hit him, causing a shiver his spine.

Sam's hands shook as he picked up the nozzle and turned to fill his gas tank. It was then that he looked down, and his heart sank. *No! Please don't tell me that . . .*

The back tire was flat. Completely flat. And judging by the chunks of rubber missing, it was obvious he'd been driving that way for a while.

No wonder the car had been acting so erratic. No wonder it had been so hard to stay on the road.

Anger built in Sam's chest, and he pounded on the car. "Piece of junk!" he shouted. "I can't believe this piece of junk."

The gas station attendant ambled out. The tall, thin man wore a black parka. He strode over to Sam with small, quick steps.

"I got a flat tire. Is there anywhere around here I can get it fixed?"

The man shrugged. "Maybe on Monday, but not tonight. Not anytime this weekend."

"Ah, man," Sam mumbled under his breath. "You've got to be kidding. Are you sure there isn't anyone you can call?"

"You not from around here?" The man walked around the car and eyed the tire.

"Nope."

"Where you from?"

"Harding." Sam lied.

"Where you headed?"

"Uh, Denver." He lied again, but he justified it by telling

himself that both places were close enough to the truth to be partially true.

"Denver's a long way. Too far to walk." The man chuckled.

"Gee, thanks." Sam rubbed his hands together, trying to warm them. "Man, I have to get to Gold—Denver. This weekend."

"Well." The man stroked his chin, ignoring the snow that blew in his face. "There is an interstate bus that stops here, right at my gas station. It goes to Los Angeles, but I'm pretty sure it stops in Denver. It won't be around for a couple of hours, but you can wait inside."

"What should I do with my car?"

The man eyed Sam. "If you promise to come back sometime next week, I suppose you can park it out back."

Sam knew he couldn't make any promises. He had no idea what would happen when he found his dad. If things went well, he hoped not to come back to Nebraska for a long time. If at all. And if things went bad . . . well, he didn't want to think about that.

"I guess I don't have a choice. It won't wreck it to drive it back there, will it?"

"Well, you can't leave it here, now can you?"

"No." Sam climbed inside and started his engine, then as slowly as he could he drove it around and parked it in back.

Sam hated the idea of leaving his car, but he hated the idea of not finding his dad even more. Sam parked the car, grabbed his things, and then headed toward the door of the small station, realizing he didn't even know the name of the town. *Where am I?* He looked around. *Just another no-good place in a no-good state.*

As his feet crunched on the snow he suddenly felt very far from home, and very alone.

Chapter Fifteen

Charlotte straightened up the house, growing excited over the thought of having her whole family together for an evening meal. It had seemed like ages since she'd seen Jennifer and Madison, and she smiled, imagining them running around the house, chasing Lightning and filling the house with giggles.

Tired of writing, Christopher had put away his notebook, and had instead decided to make Lightning a spaceship out of cardboard. He had cardboard, scissors, and duct tape scattered all over the floor next to the corn-burning stove. The warmest part of the house.

Even though she'd never thought she'd be actively parenting again, it seemed right to have the kids around, filling up the house with their interesting antics. Even though the world outside the windows was cold and dreary, the presence of her grandchildren was like filling the inside with sunshine.

Charlotte put a pan of wheat bread in the oven, knowing she'd need it for sandwiches after church the next day. Then she looked down the road, expecting Melody to be arriving any minute with Ashley.

After Emily's promise that she'd get all her chores done faster and better with Ashley's help, and with Melody agreeing to give her daughter a ride out to the farm, a sleepover had been finalized.

A few minutes later, Charlotte saw Melody's car slowly moving toward the house. Emily must have been watching from the upstairs window, because as soon as the car pulled up and stopped, Emily jogged down the stairs, sidling up to her grandmother at the window.

With her red curls bouncing, Ashley leapt from the front seat of her mom's car and swung a bright yellow duffle bag over her shoulder. Then she gave her mother a wave good-bye.

From the window, Charlotte motioned for Melody to come inside, but Melody didn't glance up. Instead, she offered a quick wave to Ashley and slowly turned the car around and headed back to town.

Emily opened the front door for her friend. "Hurry! It's freezing."

Ashley raced inside, nearly tripping on the pile of shoes by the door. "Wow, it's *really* cold out there. I mean C-O-L-D, cold." She quickly took off her jacket and hung it up.

"Where's your mom off to in such a hurry?" Charlotte asked. "I was hoping she'd come in and say hello. I wanted to gush about the wonderful meal she made for my surprise Valentine's dinner. I'm hoping Bob will make it a tradition."

Ashley giggled, "Yeah, but if it was a tradition it couldn't be a surprise, now could it?" Ashley dropped her duffle to the floor. "And, yeah, sorry my mom was in such a hurry. She and my dad are going out tonight. She was so busy cooking for everyone else last night they didn't get to do anything special."

"Well, good for them." Charlotte said, noticing the scent of her bread wafting up from the oven. "Are they going up to Harding?"

Ashley shrugged. "I don't know. I didn't ask." She walked over to the Crock-Pot of beef stew that Charlotte had started. "But wherever they go for dinner won't be as yummy as what we're going to have here. I just *love* your stew."

"Thanks, nothing special. We were going to have spaghetti, but Bill and his family are coming for dinner last minute too. It was easier throwing it together than making another trip to town for something special. And my beef stew has always been one of Bill's favorites."

And the stew is almost *gourmet if I serve it in my favorite china bowls*, Charlotte thought with a smile. She went to give the stew a stir.

In addition to being gourmet, her cooking was also mostly organic—with Charlotte growing their vegetables and using their own farm-raised beef. All of the cooking magazines she'd read lately mentioned organic food and its benefits. She never realized how *healthy* she'd been over the years. Not by choice, but by the nature of living on the farm. If not a hundred percent organic, then at least it was free-range. Charlotte chuckled to herself as she put away the freshly laundered hand towels into the drawer.

"So, are Bill, Anna, and the girls coming over tonight?" Ashley asked.

"Yep. It'll be a full house—"

"Cool. Okay." Emily interrupted, making it clear she'd shared her friend's attention long enough.

"Let us know if you need help setting the table or something later," added Ashley. Then they both turned to head upstairs to Emily's room.

"Aren't you forgetting something?" Charlotte straightened her apron.

"Chores," Emily moaned.

"Don't worry." Ashley grabbed the jacket that she'd just hung up. "We can get 'em done lickety-split."

Emily bundled herself too, and then they clung together as they headed outside, as if anchoring themselves would keep them from blowing away.

Charlotte smiled as she watched them go. She wished she had a friend to talk to as she did *her* chores. Instead, she hummed some of her favorite "oldie" tunes to herself as she finished the laundry, mopped the kitchen floor, and even cleaned out all the questionable items in the back of the fridge.

As Charlotte was finishing, she noticed Christopher was back at the table, again hard at work on his story. Toby curled at his feet. The house was quiet without the sound of the older teens or Bob's television blaring. Bob and Pete had gone to town to pick up some supplies, which she knew was their way of saying they needed to get out of the house and have some time to chat with friends at the tractor supply store. She'd noticed their anxiety as of late. It had been a long winter, and it didn't seem like it was letting up any time soon.

This happened every February—Bob would go from reading, to watching television, to checking on the animals as if he was bored and was just filling the time until spring arrived and he could be back outside again. But on days like today, spring seemed like a distant dream. Charlotte stared out at the barn and sighed, noticing the sky darkening, threatening a heavy snowfall.

She wondered how soon Pete and Bob would be back.

She hated the thought of them driving the country roads in a storm. There were too many places to get stuck, and too few people that passed that way.

Charlotte also wondered if she should call Sam at Paul's house. She hadn't heard from him, which must mean he was enjoying himself. Still, his car wasn't equipped for even the slightest snow flurry.

"Okay, Grandma. How 'bout this?" Christopher interrupted her thoughts.

"Is it a new story?" Charlotte asked.

"Yup. One you can see—in your mind, that is." Christopher tapped his temple with his fingertip.

She placed her hands on her hips. "Okay, I'm ready. Give it to me." Charlotte pulled out the chair and sat down next to Christopher. She folded the dishtowel she was carrying and placed it on her lap.

Christopher smiled as he started to read. "I walked outside. Everything was white. On the farm there are always a lot of animal footprints on the snow. This was my first winter on the farm, and it was a mystery to me what animal the footprints came from. My favorite game is to find footprints and then guess who they belong to." Christopher put down the paper. "That's the start, and then I'm going to describe them so the reader has to guess too."

"Very good. I like it. This story makes me interested right from the beginning."

Christopher's face brightened. "Good. I'll tell about the chicken and horse prints." He laughed to himself. "And then remember that time that Uncle Pete tried to trick me by rolling snowballs down the small hill by the creek? He told me the markings were the prints from a lumpy snake that had just eaten one of the chickens."

"Did he do that? I didn't hear about it, but it sounds like something Uncle Pete would do." Charlotte laughed. "It seems like you enjoy writing, Christopher."

He shrugged. "Yeah, sort of." He glanced up at her with a big grin. "Especially if you can get money for it."

"Do you know your mother liked to write too? It was one of her favorite subjects. I think it was in the fifth or sixth grade when she first started writing in a journal. She carried that thing around everywhere, jotting down notes."

Christopher nodded, and his eyes turned to the window. But Charlotte could tell his mind wasn't on the view outside. From his distant gaze she could tell he was thinking back, remembering his mom.

Charlotte's fingertips played with the fringed edge of the dishtowel as she tried to consider what to say.

"My mom liked telling stories too—not just writing them. Sometimes we'd go sit on the roof of our apartment building and she'd tell me stories."

"Oh, things about the people she met at work?"

Christopher giggled. "No, stories about made-up people—like ones who flew around the world in a hot air balloon or ones who invented shoes that could bounce you to the moon."

"Fiction." Charlotte nodded.

"Funny," Christopher said. "She—"

The door opened, and Emily and Ashley blew in.

"Okay, Grandma, all done." Emily puffed on her cold hands and then slipped off her jacket.

"Yep, all done," Ashley said, bouncing up and down as if trying to get warm.

"We're headin' upstairs to study," Ashley said with a smile, glancing in Emily's direction. From their shared looks

Charlotte could tell that homework was the last thing on their minds.

"Sounds good to me. Enjoy your, uh, studying, girls."

Then with the girls upstairs, her own chores done, and Christopher engrossed in his story, Charlotte sat down with her Bible. Even though she'd already spent time this morning with a cup of coffee, reading God's Word, Charlotte felt drawn to it again.

The truth was, Sam's recent birthday had made her think about Denise and everything around Sam's birth. Even though Denise's pregnancy had been a shock, she'd always considered Sam a special gift. It was during her waiting for her first grandchild to be born that Charlotte had found special meaning in Psalm 139. Opening the Bible on her lap, she turned to it again, reading over the message about God knowing each of us before our births, knitting us together in our mother's womb, and thinking good thoughts of us. Reading those words again warmed her even more than the corn burner. God had good plans for her grandchildren—plans that were still unfolding. Plans that she was finally settling into.

Help me, Lord, to remind these kids of this—that you knew them and created them. That you have good plans for them.

She opened her eyes and her gaze fell on Christopher.

Unaware that his grandmother was snatching a moment of her day to spend time with God, he turned to her. "Is it time for lunch yet?"

"Lunch? Oh yes, I forget. I'm sure I can come up with something."

Ten minutes later Charlotte shuffled upstairs to call the girls down for a late lunch. She peeked inside the half-open door and discovered that, as she'd figured the only thing

Emily and Ashley were studying were the photos of the boys in last year's yearbook. Charlotte paused and eyed them lying on the floor with the book open in front of them.

"Travis Hollinger is *so* cute," Ashley chattered on, "and remember that time he offered to be your lab partner? Maybe he's the one who gave you the rose."

"Maybe, but what about the other one? Someone with really messy handwriting." Emily flipped the page and scanned down. "Hmm. Maybe Knox."

"Yeah, he's cute, but this is a really bad picture of him. He looks much better in person. I'm so glad he got a better haircut."

"I *totally* agree." Emily laughed. "But even with a bad haircut he has the best smile—"

Charlotte sighed. *I started this whole thing by buying that flower.* She pressed her fingers to her temples.

Then again, she'd only given Emily one of them. Someone else *had* given that flower to Emily. Who? Charlotte hoped that, unlike the mystery in Christopher's story, this mystery wouldn't be solved. Who knew what types of trouble that would start again?

Charlotte knocked on the door and pushed it open. "Girls, I have some LTL sandwiches ready if you want to come down."

Color rose to Emily's cheeks as she realized her grandmother had most likely heard her last comment. She closed the yearbook and jumped to her feet. "Oh, my fav. I love those sandwiches. Thanks, Grams!" She shoved the yearbook under the bed with a kick of her foot.

"What's LTL?" Ashley pulled her curly red hair back from her face and fastened it with the rubber band she'd had on her wrist. Ashley offered Charlotte a sly smile and pink tinged her cheeks as she realized she too had been overheard talking about boys.

Charlotte tried to act natural. "LTL stands for lettuce, tomato, and more lettuce. It's Emily's special version since she doesn't eat meat, but I do have sliced ham in the fridge if you'd like to add some flavor to your sandwich."

"Thanks, Mrs. Stevenson." Ashley scooted past her through the door and then hurried down the stairs to the kitchen.

"Thanks, Grandma," Emily said, not making eye contact.

"Emily?" Charlotte reached out and touched her arm as she tried to brush past.

"Hmm?" Emily glanced back, tucking her blonde hair behind her ear. She bit her lip and shyly glanced at Charlotte as if expecting a lecture.

"It's okay to talk about guys—and to wonder about your flowers. I—"

Emily crossed her arms over her chest and took a step back, making it clear that this was the last thing she wanted to discuss with her grandmother.

Charlotte weighed whether she should continue, and decided she did need to say something about the roses. "Emily, I know you've probably been thinking a lot about the roses, and that's only natural. Just don't think about it so much that you can't think about anything else."

"Yeah, okay, thanks, Grandma." Emily's brow wrinkled as if she was wondering if she should say something more. She took a step forward, then she paused and turned back. "Are we done?"

"I suppose so. Unless you had something you needed to talk to me about?"

Emily glanced down toward the kitchen and then back to Charlotte. "Just one question, I suppose."

Charlotte nodded. "Sure."

"Uh, did you have crushes when you were my age?" Emily asked.

Charlotte laughed. "My, yes, and every girl does. Yet the important thing is to realize the emotions can get us into trouble if we're not careful, and—" Charlotte caught herself. Emily didn't need a lecture, not today. Not with her friend hanging out at the bottom of the stairs. "And you better get that sandwich before your lettuce gets warm." Charlotte smiled.

Emily looked relieved. Then she bounded down the stairs.

Charlotte noticed Sam's bedroom door was cracked open. She walked over to close it, knowing how crazy he got when Lightning got into his stuff. She reached the door and paused, looking in. It was clean—cleaner than she'd ever seen it. And empty, as if he'd put everything away, out of sight. It seemed as if it had been weeks, not just one day, since Sam had been gone.

An anxious feeling overcame her, but Charlotte pushed it out of her mind. Sam had just spent the night at a friend's house. He was fine. And he would be home soon.

Charlotte turned and noticed Christopher had planted himself on the bottom of the stairs. His head was cocked, and as he sat there he seemed to be listening to the girls' conversation.

Charlotte let her fingers glide over the handrail as she moved down the stairs toward him. "Hey there, bud, what are you up to?"

"Oh, just thinking." He scratched his chin with the pink eraser on the pencil. "You know, there might be more interesting things to write about around here than animal tracks." He eyed his sister and Ashley.

Charlotte crossed her arms over her chest. "I don't think so. That's the last thing your sister needs—to have her crushes broadcast all over the elementary school."

"Crushes?"

"Yes, the boys she likes."

Christopher looked disappointed. "Okay, I won't write about crushes."

The ringing of the phone split the air, and Charlotte hurried down the stairs.

"I got it!" Emily lunged for the phone. "Hello?" She walked back toward her sandwich, the phone cord stretching behind her.

"Yes, this is Emily." She stopped midstep. "Oh, hi *Hunter*." Her voice raised an octave as she said his name.

"Hunter?" Ashley mumbled with a bite of sandwich in her mouth. She put down her sandwich and gave Emily two thumbs-up.

Charlotte paused beside Ashley. She leaned close to the red-headed girl and realized she smelled like apple shampoo. "Who's Hunter?"

Ashley shrugged. "Oh, just a guy from school—in our own grade. His parents bought the old Schnurnberger place right down the road. He's nice."

One minute later Emily hung up the phone. "That's so cool. Hunter is riding his horse down."

"Down where?" Charlotte eyed the mounting clouds outside the window.

"Down here. He lives right down the road. His dad just bought—"

"The old Schnurnberger place, I know, but don't you think you should ask before you invite someone over? You already have a friend here, and your aunt, uncle, and cousins are coming for dinner," Charlotte said. "Besides, have you seen the weather? It's already starting to snow."

"Oh, uh, I didn't think of that. Hunter just said he was riding down. We'll hang out in the barn, and I'll make sure he doesn't stay long." Emily twisted the cord of the phone around her finger. "Besides, remember at church last Sunday, Hannah was telling you about the family. She said they were really nice."

"You're right, she did say that. Although Hannah seems to like everyone." Charlotte spotted Bob's truck rumbling down the driveway, and she felt a sense of relief. The back-up had arrived. She could always count on Bob to get the kids to take care of what they needed to.

"So, fine, but Hunter doesn't need to stay very long." Charlotte waved to Bob, now climbing out of the truck, and then she turned back to Emily. She tried to appear nonchalant as she prepared to ask the next question. "So do you think Hunter is the one who gave you a rose? And maybe Knox the other?"

"Or, maybe Hunter gave Emily *both*, and he just had someone else write the note for him," Ashley piped up. "It's possible, you know."

"I don't know about both. Weren't there two cards by two different people?" Charlotte asked. Charlotte let out a slow breath, hoping she didn't appear suspicious. The aroma of beef stew filled her nostrils. She removed the lid and stirred the stew, hoping that Emily didn't suspect her.

Emily shrugged. "I dunno. I mean, we don't know for sure that Knox gave me one. It was just a guess. So maybe one was from Hunter."

"Or, like I said before, maybe both were from Hunter,

and he just had a friend write the second card for him." Ashley pointed a finger in the air. "That would be smart."

"Yes, well. Just make sure Hunter doesn't stay long. He's new to the area and he may not be aware of how quickly storms blow in. Speaking of which, I need to call Sam."

"Yeah, where is Sam?" Ashley asked. Then she took a big bite of her sandwich. She chewed it slowly and then swallowed. "I, uh, thought he was going to be here today." Charlotte noted the disappointment in the girl's gaze.

"He's at his friend Paul's house."

Ashley took another bite. "Is he going to be back soon?" she said from the side of her mouth.

"Yes, I sure hope so. Why?"

"Oh. Just wondering," Ashley said with the slightest hint of a smile.

As the girls finished eating their lunch, Charlotte made a sandwich for Christopher. With the three kids fed, Charlotte thought she'd check on the fourth. She tried Sam's cell phone but it went straight to voice mail.

Charlotte sighed. "He probably forgot to charge it again. What am I going to do with that kid?"

I suppose I'll have to look up the number for Paul's house.

She looked up Paul's parents' phone number in the phonebook. Charlotte dialed, but there was a busy signal. Outside, Bob and Pete were unloading the truck, and their eyes were fixed on something down the road. Hoping it was Sam's car they were focused on, Charlotte followed their gaze. Instead, she saw that it was a young man—who she assumed was Hunter—riding down the driveway on a large black stallion.

Charlotte neared the window and craned her neck to get

a better look. Cold air radiated off the glass, and she felt a shiver travel up her spine. "How in the world did he get here so fast?"

Emily wrinkled her nose, and a sly grin spread across her face. "He, uh, called from his cell phone." She tossed half of her lettuce sandwich into the garbage and then hurried toward the back door and quickly put on her coat and winter boots.

"Oh my gosh, that is so cool," Ashley squealed as she slid her arms into her jacket. She took one last bite of her sandwich and then tossed her napkin in the trash. Then, before Charlotte could respond, the girls darted out the door.

"Well, I've heard everything now," Charlotte shook her head. "Making a cell phone call on horseback—"

She heard a giggle behind her and noticed Christopher watching her from the kitchen table. He rested his elbows on his knees, and his chin rested on his hands. Instead of running to the window to see what the new neighbor boy was up to, he seemed content to watch Charlotte.

Their gazes locked, and Christopher sighed. "Grandma, are you *sure* I can't write about this?"

HUNTER SEEMED like a nice enough boy, or at least from what Charlotte could tell from a distance. She watched as the three teens took his horse into the barn, and she imagined what Bob thought about that. Everyone knew the barn was his territory. Even when Pete did his best to maintain things on the farm, not a day went by when Bob didn't go back after his son and try to fix things *just right*.

Pete took some packages to his apartment. The first thing Charlotte noticed when Bob came back into the house was that he was whistling. And instead of complaining about the teens and the horse, Bob seemed impressed with the horse and its owner.

"That's no 4-H pony, that's for sure." Bob settled down into his recliner and flipping on the television. "That horse is worth more than my truck, Pete's truck, *and* Sam's car put together."

"Maybe, but that's not saying much." Charlotte glanced at the clock. "Speaking of Sam, I think I'll try him again." She picked up the phone and dialed Paul's home number again. There was still a busy signal. Again Charlotte tried to ignore the nagging feeling that something was going on with Sam. Everyone else seemed to be getting on with their day, so why was she getting anxious? Sometimes she wondered if her brain purposely tried to come up with things for her to worry about. It wasn't as if Sam was a first grader. In fact, when she was his age she would often drive up to Harding with friends and spend the whole day up there without checking in once.

Charlotte pushed all worries of Sam out of her mind. "Bill and Anna are coming for dinner. Did I tell you?"

"Yup, three times." Bob focused on the television game show as if it was the most interesting thing in the world. "It will be good to see 'em. Winter makes it hard to spend much time together. Hope the roads are okay."

She thought through her menu. Homemade beef stew, Anna's salad, fresh biscuits—which she still had to make. She also knew she needed something colorful for dessert. Maybe a Jell-O cake? Not quite gourmet, but the kids always loved those.

Thinking about her high school years over the last couple of days had made her realize how much her home economics training had stuck with her. For example, the idea of making meals colorful. Her teacher taught her the color wheel of meal prep as diligently as if she'd been teaching art. *Something brown, something green, something red or yellow.* In recent years kids were taught more useful stuff such as the nutritional content of foods.

Charlotte smiled as she remembered some of her teacher's other favorite phrases: "You are sewing with a railroad spike" and, "Your thread is long enough to go to Kansas City and back." Those were the days.

Charlotte chuckled. Bob didn't seem to be paying her any mind. On the blaring television, the contestant missed the last question and lost the prize money. Bob mumbled under this breath, and then flipped off the TV. He lumbered into the kitchen.

"Oh, the kids told me to tell you they'd be inside in a few. Got any cookies and cocoa around here?" He shuffled to the cookie jar on the counter and opened it to find just a few crumbs on the bottom.

"You asking for them, or for you?" Charlotte placed her hands on her hips.

"For them, of course." Bob grinned and patted his large paunch.

"Yes, that's what I thought." Charlotte grinned back.

Teenage laughter filled the air and a minute later Emily, Ashley, and a young man were stomping their way inside.

"Grandma, this is Hunter," Emily said, looking a little shy. "Grandpa's already met him."

"Hello, Hunter. Nice to meet you," Charlotte said as she reluctantly pulled out store-bought cookies she'd gotten for school lunches.

"Hello, Mrs. Stevenson. Thank you for letting me, uh, drop by," said Hunter, standing stiffly.

When the kids sat down, Hunter sat between the girls. They bookended him, their light skin and lighter shades of hair contrasting with Hunter's handsome dark looks.

Instead of going upstairs to change the sheets on the kids' beds as she'd planned, Charlotte hung around the kitchen, keeping her eyes on the driveway, watching for Sam and listening with interest to Hunter's fantastic stories. He wove a tale of his last barrel-racing win in a way that transfixed even her.

"The thing about barrel racing is that it's best if you can be one of the first ones to go," Hunter said.

"Why's that?" Emily asked. She sat close to Hunter, but not too close. She also talked to him in an even tone and with real interest, so different from the giggly way she talked about boys she had crushes on.

"Well, when you're one of the first ones, the ground is perfectly raked and even, but then with each racer the horses' hoofs create a worn path in the ground. This path trips up the horses that follow and slows them down. It takes a lot of work to place when you're one of the last riders."

"I'd like to see you ride sometime," Emily commented, breaking off a piece of cookie with her fingers. "It does sound sort of interesting."

"Well, I'm sure you can come down and watch me train. Or—if you want to see a competition—you can come and watch the rodeo at the county fair at the end of summer."

"Sure. I'd like that." Emily took a sip from her cocoa. "So when did you start racing?"

Hunter launched into another story, and Bob approached

Charlotte, leaning in close. "I wonder whether he's one good cowboy, or one good storyteller," Bob mumbled in Charlotte's ear as he rinsed out his mug.

"Well, either way he has the girls' attention," Charlotte said. Then she turned her attention back to the teens, realizing Hunter reminded her of a young John Travolta.

She moved closer to Bob, and he leaned down so she could whisper in his ear. "I can't tell if he likes Emily or Ashley, or both. Or neither."

"And that's a bad thing?" Bob asked. "He's a nice kid; why do they have to pair up? They're too young for that. Too young to even think about dating."

Yet five minutes later, when Hunter returned outside to saddle up his horse and head home, it was Emily who accompanied him. But instead of acting jealous, Ashley smiled as she set three mugs in the sink and rinsed them out.

"Do you need help mixing that dough?" Ashley watched as Charlotte finished adding the ingredients for biscuits into the bowl.

"I'm fine. Why don't you join Emily and Hunter outside?"

"Well, for one thing it's cold. And for another thing I think Hunter's nice but—if I have to hear another barrel-racing story I think I'll scream." She chuckled to herself. "Really, I can cut that dough for you if you'd like. My mom taught me how."

Charlotte handed the bowl to Ashley. "Well, despite his storytelling, Hunter seems like an interesting boy."

"Yeah, I think so, although Emily likes him more as a friend than anything else." Ashley cut the dough with a fork and then paused to grab another cookie from the package and pop it in her mouth.

"That may mean he likes Emily even more than she likes him. I wonder if one of the flowers was from him."

"Could be," Ashley said with a shrug of her shoulders. Then she scooted next to Charlotte and lowered her voice. "Can you keep a secret?"

"Sure." Charlotte glanced over her shoulder to make sure Christopher wasn't anywhere close. That kid seemed to have bionic hearing. Then she leaned her ear closer to Ashley.

"I bought her one of those roses. I just wanted to make sure she got one, you know. But I suppose I shouldn't have been too worried."

"*You* did?" Charlotte hoped she sounded surprised. She also didn't know whether to feel sad for Emily, or relieved. Sad that her roses were from her grandmother and best friend. Or relieved because of the same.

Chapter
Sixteen

Bob, do you think we should drive into town?" Charlotte glanced at the clock, noting it was nearly 4:00 PM. She had tried to call Sam's cell phone and Paul's house three more times, but she still hadn't gotten through.

"Sam should be home soon. I'd hate to drive in and waste all that gas."

Charlotte wasn't sure. She walked over to the kitchen sink and looked out at the falling snow. Crossing her arms over her chest, she leaned back against the kitchen counter. Scents of dinner wafted through the air, but instead of anticipation, tightness squeezed her chest. Here she was safe and warm, and who knew what Sam was doing—or where he was? The memory of his downcast attitude over the last few weeks filled her thoughts.

"But what if his car is broken down somewhere? The temperature's dropping fast. And you know Sam. I'm lucky if I can get him to wear a sweatshirt. I don't think he's worn his winter jacket even once since we got it for him."

The ringing of the phone split the air, making Charlotte jump.

"Finally," she mumbled as she cradled the phone between her shoulder and cheek. "Hello?" Charlotte attempted to keep her voice calm.

"Mrs. Stevenson? It's Anita Marshall, Paul's mother. I saw your phone number on my caller ID from earlier today. Did you try to call?"

"Oh good. I'm glad you're home. Please call me Charlotte. Yes, I called a few times. I don't mean to be such a pest, but I was wondering—did Sam already leave, or is he going to be heading home soon? We just want to watch out for him—that car of his is always giving him trouble."

"Sam?" Anita's voice sounded hesitant. "Well, he did stay last night, but he left this morning. Sam said he wasn't feeling well. Personally, I wouldn't feel well either if I stayed up all night eating junk food and playing video games."

"He left your house this morning?" Charlotte felt the pit of her stomach sinking. The room around her began to fade and she leaned back against the kitchen counter for support.

"Yes, hours ago. And after he left, Paul and Jake headed out back to snowboard. Do you think Sam might have stopped by another friend's house?"

"No, I'm afraid not . . . I mean, Paul and Jake are the only ones he really hangs out with. He promised to call before he left."

She felt her throat closing and pain shot through her chest. She remembered that feeling well. It had been the same the day she discovered that Denise had run away with Kevin Slater.

Sam didn't run away, she told herself. *He . . . he has just chosen not to come home yet. Either that or—*

Charlotte hoped he wasn't stuck out there somewhere. She glanced toward the window, noticing the snow falling hard.

From somewhere beyond Anita's voice, Charlotte heard a car driving down their driveway—the snow crunching under the tires. She turned her head quickly, hoping it was Sam pulling in. Instead, she saw that Bill, Anna, and the girls had arrived early.

Toby barked by the back door, wanting to be let out. The sound of Christopher's footsteps pounded down the stairs. Then Emily's and Ashley's faces darted by as they followed Christopher.

Emily's cheeks were flushed as she let in Bill's family, and Charlotte attempted to make sense of it all.

"Charlotte? Hello? Are you there? Did we lose connection—" It was Anita's voice pulling her back to the conversation on the phone.

Charlotte pressed the phone tighter to her ear. "Maybe you're right, Anita. I'm sure Sam is at another friend's house, and he just forgot to let me know."

Then a new memory filtered into Charlotte's thoughts, and she remembered the last time she saw Sam. He was carrying a garbage bag of items out the door. Sam had told her he'd cleaned his room and was throwing out trash, getting everything in order. But what if he'd been packing up his things? Packing up for good?

He didn't want to leave the room a mess for me. He wasn't planning on coming back.

"Charlotte, are you still there?" Anita's voice asked.

"Charlotte." Bob approached and stood in front of her. "Did you see that the kids are here? Should Anna set the salad on the table, or put it in the fridge?" He leaned down, his eyes meeting with hers. "Charlotte, who are you talking to?"

Charlotte motioned to the table. "Put the salad there," she mouthed. Even with Anita's voice in her ear she had a hard time connecting the woman's words with the normal family interactions happening around her.

Bob shrugged. He said something to Anna that Charlotte couldn't make out, and then he moved into the living room with Bill.

"Charlotte?" Anita said again into the phone.

"Yes, I'm sorry, I'm still here." Charlotte managed to focus on the woman's voice.

"The weather's not getting any better out there. We need to act fast. That's a long time for Sam to be gone, and I'll do what I can to help. I'll call a few of Paul's friends and see if anyone knows anything. Maybe you'd better call the sheriff's office, let them know what's going on. Find out how long someone has to be gone before you can file a missing person report—"

Charlotte didn't know what else to do but to listen and agree to the plan. "Okay, yes, you're right."

It was Anna who first figured out something was wrong. She had just set a large, glass bowl filled with a fresh and lovely salad on the table when her eyes met Charlotte's gaze.

"Sam," Anna mouthed. Charlotte nodded.

"Okay, Charlotte?" It was Anita's voice interrupting again.

"Yes, okay, Anita, thank you. I appreciate your looking for him. I'm sure he'll show up around town somewhere."

Charlotte said the words even though she didn't believe them herself. "Thank you. Good-bye." She hung up.

Her eyes began to water. That old sports car wasn't made

for Nebraska winters. And deep down she knew the truth . . . Sam wasn't at a friend's house. Sam was gone, just as Denise had gone.

She thought about Sam, stranded and alone. At least Denise had left with someone who had watched out for her—at least for a while. As frustrating as Kevin Slater could be, there was a time when he had given up everything to care for Denise.

But Sam was alone. Completely alone. *Where? Why? And why now?*

"Dad," Anna's voice called across the house to the living room. Charlotte vaguely realized it was the first time she'd heard her daughter-in-law shout so unladylike. "Dad, come quick. There's a problem with Sam."

Anna knelt down before her. "Mom?"

"Charlotte? What's going on?" Bob's hand touched her shoulder. Bill stood behind him.

Charlotte took in a deep breath and blew it out slowly.

"It seems that Sam left Paul's house this morning. No one knows where he is. But I'm sure he just forgot he was supposed to call home. I'm sure it was just a misunderstanding."

"He's missing?" Bob's eyebrows furrowed as if he was having a hard time believing it.

"Grandma?" It was Christopher who stood before her, stretching out his hand. In it was a roll of new toilet paper. "Here, Grandma. You can wipe your face with this." His face wrinkled in concern.

"Is Sam all right? Did someone take him? Will he be back?" Christopher's questions stabbed her heart.

Charlotte took the toilet paper from him, and then stroked his cheek. Still, her mind seemed muffled and she tried to make sense of why Christopher was handing her toilet paper.

"For your tears, Mom. Wipe *your* face." Anna took the roll from her, unrolling it and breaking off a piece.

Charlotte took it and dabbed her face. "For my tears. Yes, I'm sorry." A forced laugh escaped her lips. "I'm sorry," she said again. "I didn't know I was crying."

She grabbed Bob's hand, trying to keep her voice measured. "We need to call the sheriff. We need to call now, Bob. Sam's out there somewhere—and we need to find him!"

WE NEED TO FIND HIM . . . The words replayed in Charlotte's mind as she and Bob followed the sheriff's deputy into Sam's room.

Seeing him there, eyeing Sam's things, looked like something she'd watched in a movie once. The authorities had been alerted to check every possible route Sam could have taken to get home from Paul's house. But from the quick response of a deputy showing up at their farm, asking to see Sam's room, Charlotte guessed that they didn't believe Sam was lost or broken down, especially when she told them that most of Sam's things were missing.

Just like she didn't believe it.

This can't be reality. It can't be real. I wish I could wake up from this. I wish it was just a bad dream.

When Charlotte had first opened the door she was surprised by the youthfulness of the deputy's appearance. Just a few inches taller than Charlotte, he had a thin build, sandy blond hair, and kind eyes. Yet as he gazed around Sam's room, his eyes narrowed and she could see him taking it all in.

His ID badge said Johnson. Charlotte didn't know him, and she was thankful for that. Thankful that the man who stood before her wasn't one of the old-timers who knew about Denise. She didn't know if she could handle that—all those memories—and maybe even accusations. After all, how often did this type of thing happen twice in the same family?

She was glad the deputy had suggested the others stay downstairs. Bob had protested, but Charlotte had assured him that it was a good idea. Even now she could hear the members of her family discussing where Sam could have gone and why. It was hard enough for Charlotte having the deputy here, asking questions, without a dozen prying eyes watching, observing and adding their own opinions.

"So, you say his duffle bag and most of his clothes are missing?" Deputy Johnson asked. He jotted a few notes in his small white notebook and then he turned, his eyes locking on hers with sympathy.

"Yes, as well as a few of his favorite things, including his Bible." The fact that Sam took his Bible had been one small encouragement to Charlotte.

"Did he have any money?" The deputy continued to jot down notes with the intensity of a college student copying chemistry equations from a white board.

"Not much, at least I don't think he did. Well, he did get a little bit for his birthday. Maybe forty dollars. Maybe a little more."

"Is there any other money lying around that he could have gotten his hands on? Maybe from a wallet or a purse?"

Charlotte frowned, and Deputy Johnson put down his pen. "I'm sorry to ask these questions, ma'am. I know this is hard. Just realize that my goal isn't to place any accusations on your grandson—it will simply help us create a better picture of Sam's resources."

"Sam might be difficult sometimes, but stealing money isn't like him," she stammered.

Then again, neither is running away—

"What about the grocery money?" the deputy asked.

"Yes, well, I do keep grocery money in my purse. I suppose I can go check," she said simply.

She hurried downstairs, eager to get to her purse and disprove the assumption.

The eyes of the other family members followed Charlotte as she moved through the living room to her bedroom. Their conversation quieted. Charlotte didn't make eye contact, didn't comment. Instead, she walked into her bedroom where she kept her purse and unzipped the front pocket. Her heart sank. It was empty. The cash for her weekly grocery shopping was gone. Feeling another weight added to those she already carried, Charlotte settled onto her bed, placing her forehead into her hands.

Dear Lord, help us here. She needed a few minutes to think, to pray. To let the seriousness of this situation sink in.

From the dining room she could hear the sound of dishes rattling as Bill and Anna set the table for the kids. They had all been unsure of what to do or how to act, so Anna had taken charge. Before the deputy had arrived, Anna had made it clear that she thought it would be best if they all tried to keep the kids' routine as close to normal so as not to shake them up. Charlotte didn't know if it was the right thing or not, but she didn't want to argue.

As Charlotte sat there, listening to them say grace and praying that God would protect Sam—wherever he might be—she tried to regain her composure. And as she heard them dishing up food and exclaiming over the meal, she couldn't help but think about Sam. Alone somewhere, maybe even hungry and cold.

Taking in a slow breath, Charlotte exited her room. She glanced at her family, sitting around the table, but didn't say anything. She knew if she tried to speak tears would tumble out with the words. Instead, she offered a forced smile, and then she hurried back upstairs. Bob rose from the table and followed her.

Deputy Johnson turned as they approached. He lifted his eyebrows as if already guessing what Charlotte had to tell him.

"There was two hundred dollars of grocery money in my purse. It's missing."

Bob's hand gently squeezed Charlotte's shoulder. "Oh, Sam," he mumbled.

Deputy Johnson simply nodded, and Charlotte was glad he didn't do any more than that. Even though they were finding out more and more of his discrepancies by the minute, he was still her grandson and she loved him fiercely.

"So, he didn't say anything about wanting to run away? And there was no note?" the deputy asked.

"No, I haven't seen anything. He's just gone." Charlotte held her fingers to her trembling lips.

"If it's okay, I'd like to talk to Sam's brother and sister. They might know more than they let on."

Charlotte nodded. "Bob?" She didn't need to ask. Bob went to go get the children. A minute later Emily and Christopher were sitting on Sam's bed with the deputy kneeling down in front of them. *So much for trying not to rattle them.*

The deputy asked Christopher the same types of questions—

if Sam had said anything, if he'd done anything out of the ordinary . . .

Christopher shrugged. "No, I don't think so. He was just the same ol' Sam."

The deputy turned to Emily, whose tears spilled from her eyes before she could say one word. "I could tell something was wrong, but I didn't know what. Sam has never done anything like this before. Ever."

Deputy Johnson finished looking over the room and did a walk-through of the rest of the house. As he prepared to leave, he approached Bob and Charlotte. "I can put out an APB for him."

Charlotte nodded, but the words didn't bring her any comfort.

"I do have one last question," Deputy Johnson stated. "Do you know the whereabouts of his father? What was his name?"

"Kevin Slater, and we haven't heard from the man for years, not since he abandoned his family. If we did know his whereabouts, you'd be the first to know." Bob's voice was deep, full of the emotion that name stirred.

"We tried to find him—after our daughter's death." Charlotte met the deputy's gaze. "But we weren't able to locate him. We haven't heard from him in years. The kids haven't either."

Deputy Johnson nodded. "I promise to call in Sam's description to state authorities, and I'll keep you updated if I hear anything. I suppose all you can do is just try to think back—even to look around—to see if anything strikes you as unusual. It's often the little things that lead to our biggest breaks."

Bob and Charlotte nodded in unison, not knowing what else to say. They walked Deputy Johnson to the front door and then, with resignation, Charlotte turned her attention back to the family at hand.

Much to Jennifer and Madison's approval, Anna and Bill had put on *Veggie Tales* while the rest of them circled the table. Ashley had called her mom and had gone home, promising to contact some of their friends at school to see if anyone had seen Sam.

Charlotte's gaze moved from her hands to Bob's face and then to Christopher and Emily.

"It will be okay; we'll find your brother," she told them. Charlotte only wished she believed those words.

She then turned her gaze to Bill and Anna. There was a mix of sympathy and disapproval in their gazes. It made Charlotte think back to old conversations they had about who would be the best ones to raise Sam, Emily, and Christopher. Charlotte only hoped that this situation wouldn't resurrect those questions once again.

"I'm sure Sam will be fine," Bill said. "But after we find him it would be a good time to talk . . ." He cleared his throat. "I just want you to know that if you need some help—perhaps if Christopher and Emily need to stay with us for a while— we'd be very happy to do that for you."

"There will be no discussion of Emily and Christopher going anywhere—"

Bob's words were interrupted by Pete bolting through the door, rubbing his hands together. "Hey, sorry I'm late. Dana's grandma's pipe under her sink froze and burst and I had to run over there and help her get it fixed . . ." Pete paused as he glanced at the faces at the table.

"Pete—" Charlotte tried to speak, but the words caught in her throat.

"What's going on?"

"It's Sam," Bob commented. "It seems like he's run away. He's gone, and no one seems to know where he is."

"Run away?" Harsh laughter burst from Pete's lips. "You're joking, right? In his little car? As if he could make it out of Nebraska." Pete paused. "Wait, are you serious? Like seriously serious?"

"Yes, Pete. I'm afraid so."

Then, even before Bob had finished explaining everything to Pete, the phone rang. It was Anita Marshall on the phone again.

"I'm sorry, Charlotte. We've called all Paul's friends—and a few other kids from school too. None of them claim to know anything about Sam's disappearance."

"Thank you, Anita. I appreciate all your help. Please let me know if you hear anything. Maybe Sam will call Paul or Jake. And I'll do the same if we have any news."

Pete had barely taken off his jacket when he put it on again. "Has anyone just driven around—you know, around town—to see if they've spotted his car?"

"Well, the sheriff's deputies were going to keep their eyes open." Charlotte rose.

"I can't just sit here and do nothing." Pete placed his hand on the doorknob. "I'm going to drive around myself—just in case."

Charlotte felt like hugging her youngest son. *Finally, some action and not just talk.*

"Thank you, Pete. Be careful," she said as Pete exited. She watched from the window, but before the taillights on

Pete's truck, Lazarus, had disappeared, Bill and Anna were also putting on their own jackets and bundling up the girls.

"You heading out too?" Charlotte turned to Anna.

Anna approached and took Charlotte's hands in her own. "Bill doesn't want the girls to miss their bedtime. But won't you call us and let us know what's happening?"

"Yes, keep us posted." Bill sidled up to Anna. "I'll be back first thing tomorrow. I want to talk to Mom and Dad a bit." His voice was low, but firm. "Maybe Emily and Christopher should head to bed too. Children need order, structure. Things are different these days. Things we may think of as little things like bedtime schedules and routines are actually important," Bill said as he tugged on his coat. "Kids often need more guidance than we think they do."

Charlotte nodded as she led them to the door, and she knew this conversation wasn't about bedtime. It was never about bedtime. It was about Bill's opinion on who should raise the kids—and a clear statement that he didn't think Bob and Charlotte were the right choice.

Maybe Bill's right. Are we just being selfish? Maybe we should think otherwise, think of the kids. Maybe if we'd let Bill and Anna raise them this would never have happened.

Maybe this is my fault. After all, what other mothers out there have this happen twice?

~ Chapter
Seventeen

The phone rang continually throughout the evening, and never with good news.

"My guess is that you should check with the bus station in Harding in the morning." Deputy Johnson's voice was gentle. "That's the best mode of transportation out of the area. We sent information up there for the police to look for Sam's car, but don't hold your breath. The storm blowing in has caused a power outage in Harding and they're dealing with a minor crisis up there. Best thing to do is just call the station yourself in the morning, and ask them a few questions. Sometimes they'll do more to help family members than if a deputy calls."

"Okay, thank you very much. I'll do that." Yet Charlotte's words weren't nearly as agreeable when she spoke to Bob after hanging up the phone.

"Bob, there has to be more that we can do. Maybe we should drive up to Harding ourselves. Tonight."

Bob pointed to the window. "In this weather? Charlotte, it's just not safe." He wrapped an arm around her shoulders. "Don't worry. Sam may be confused, but he's not stupid.

He's not going to do anything to put his life in danger. Just the fact that he took time to pack and to make sure he didn't leave any clues behind proves he wasn't being hasty. He has a plan. Now we just need to figure out what that is."

"You're right. We'll wait for tomorrow, and in the meantime pray for his safety." She moved to the couch and settled into the cushions. Having been through this before, she knew there was nothing much they could do except wait and pray. Nothing anyone could do.

Charlotte glanced at the clock and her jaw dropped when she noticed it was after 10:00 PM. Her stomach growled, and she realized she never did get any of that stew. Not that she could eat now. Her eyelids felt heavy, and all that she could think about was sleep—to escape into a dreamland where everyone was safe and accounted for.

Bob yawned and rose, moving into the kitchen. It was only then that she realized that Emily and Christopher were sitting in the dim light, watching, listening, and not saying a word.

Charlotte got up too. "I think it's time for all of us to head to bed. Tomorrow, no doubt, will be a long day."

Christopher hesitantly moved toward her. Charlotte opened her arms to him and he fell into her embrace.

"Grandma, is Sam all right?"

"I'm sure he is. It's scary, but God is with him. We need to remember that. We need to pray for your brother."

"Can we pray now?" Emily whispered. Charlotte saw that her eyes were red and her face splotchy.

"Of course." Bob stepped forward, placing his big hands on his granddaughter's thin shoulders. "I'm not sure why we didn't think of that sooner. It should have been the first thing we did."

They circled together, in a small cluster, and Bob wrapped his big arms around them all.

"Dear Lord Jesus. We come to you with humble hearts. We don't know where Sam is, but we are thankful you do. Please be with him. Keep your eyes on him, and . . ." Bob's voice caught in his throat. "Remind him of our love. Amen."

"Amen." Charlotte said.

"Amen." Christopher and Emily echoed. But for the next minute no one moved. It was as if they all wanted to feel each other's closeness for just a little longer.

"Grandpa?" It was Emily's voice that broke the silence. "Can we sleep in the living room tonight?"

"Of course." Bob answered. "Why don't you bring down some sleeping bags." Then he turned to Charlotte and placed a hand on her shoulder. "Why don't you head to bed. I'm going to head out and check the animals, and then I'll be right in."

"You sure?" Charlotte struggled to hold back a yawn. Her eyes felt thick and scratchy, and the idea of washing her face with a warm washcloth and then snuggling down under her comforter sounded good.

"Okay, but if Pete has any news be sure to let me know."

"Will do." Bob placed a peck on Charlotte's forehead. "Now you get some rest. Tomorrow will be a new day." Then, with a slowness in his movements and a heaviness in his steps, Bob put on his coat and stocking cap and then headed outside.

Five minutes later Charlotte settled into bed. This morning she'd awakened like it was any other day. By tonight everything had changed.

She'd left the bedroom door open as a sign to Emily and Christopher that they could come in if they needed her.

But it was also Charlotte's way of feeling close to the kids. It helped to know they were just in the other room. Even now she could hear them whispering between themselves.

She was almost asleep when she heard Pete come in.

"Uncle Pete, did you see anything?" Christopher asked. She heard him jump up from his sleeping bag. She listened to the sounds of his feet running across the room toward his uncle.

Charlotte climbed out of bed and slid on her bathrobe, wondering the same question. She started down the hall to the living room and then paused.

"Sorry, buddy," Pete's voice was filled with sadness. "I drove up and down every street in Bedford—and along many of the country roads too, but there was no sign of your brother."

"Oh, Uncle Pete, where do you think he is?" Emily sighed loudly.

"I don't have any idea, but God knows. He sees Sam exactly where he is this very moment. And you know what? Sam's a pretty smart kid. Running away might not be the smartest thing, but I'm sure he had a plan."

"So you think he's going to be okay?" Christopher asked.

"Yup, I sure do. Maybe tomorrow he'll even call and let us know where he is and what he's been up to. But I have a feeling that wherever that is he'll also realize that it's not as great as being here with us."

Charlotte peeked around the corner, into the living room and noticed Pete lying down on the floor with the kids. It warmed her heart, and she returned to her room not wanting to intrude on their special moment.

Sliding between the sheets Charlotte felt as if she was

made of lead. Closing her eyes, her body pressed into the mattress, and for a moment she worried that she'd never be able to move again. Especially if something happened to Sam. She couldn't imagine life going on without him. How could Emily and Christopher cope? How could she?

She tried to pray, but the words didn't come. Instead, another voice filled her head—her own. *Failure, failure, failure*, the voice chanted. Not only did she fail once—she did it twice. Even with knowing all she knew about Denise's teenage runaway experience, she still couldn't get it right.

"Dear Lord, help me. You brought these children to us for a reason. Help me to hold them close to my heart, but hold them loosely too. They belong to you, not me . . ."

And with that prayer she felt her body relax and sleep overcome her.

Chapter Eighteen

P ain shooting through her temples stirred Charlotte from her sleep, and it took only a second for yesterday's events to come back. She sat up and turned toward Bob, but even in the dim light she saw that he wasn't there. She glanced at the alarm clock, which read nearly 6:00 AM. His side of the bed was still neatly made, which meant that Bob hadn't come to bed.

Sam. Is there any news on Sam?

She pulled on her slippers and then hurried out of the bedroom. Bob was sitting at the table close to the phone. He'd laid his head on his folded arms and had fallen asleep like that. She walked up to him wondering if she should wake him or let him sleep.

"Dad's been there all night—didn't want to leave the phone."

It was Pete. She turned and noticed him curled up on the couch. It struck her how many times he had slept on that couch like that, and no matter how well she'd tucked him in he'd always kicked the afghan off. Now that very afghan looked like a handkerchief spread over a giant. How mature a man he was now.

On the floor in front of the sofa, Christopher and Emily slept.

"Any news?" Charlotte folded her arms over her chest.

"Well, no good news. When I was driving around I called Brad. It seems Sam didn't show up for work all of last week. Brad said before that, everything was going just fine. It was like one day Sam just gave up trying."

"Maybe it was his birthday that triggered things, the first without his mom . . ." Charlotte's voice was no more than a whisper. She wanted to make sure she didn't wake the kids.

Pete shrugged. "Could be, but I have a feeling it's more than that."

"Do you think he's headed to California?"

"That I don't know."

"At least Denise left a note. I have no idea where we can even start looking for Sam."

Pete nodded and didn't say anything, then he rubbed his eyes. "It's too early to start making calls again. Why don't you try to rest a little longer."

Charlotte nodded and returned to her room, but instead of returning to bed she walked to her closet and turned her attention to the top shelf. There were three shoe boxes, and she reached up and took down the one that said *Denise*. Since her daughter's death, she hadn't had the strength to go through the box, but Sam's disappearance stirred up all the old memories, and she wanted to remember again.

Inside, Charlotte took an envelope from the top and set it to the side, and then she looked through the other items— elementary school report cards, craft projects made with yarn and coffee filters, and some pictures Denise had drawn. Her favorite was a drawing that Denise had made her first week of kindergarten. It was of Charlotte in the garden surrounded by melons and carrots and pea pods. The only reason Charlotte had known it was her was because Denise had drawn the red and blue apron on the stick figure, just like the one Charlotte had always worn. And on the top the teacher had written these words in quotes: "My favorite place to be."

Charlotte put all the items back, her chest filled with longing for her daughter, and then turned her attention back to the first envelope. It was the last thing Charlotte had tucked in the box—the letter Denise left, telling Charlotte she was pregnant with Kevin Slater's baby and was off to start her own life.

Charlotte pressed the letter to her chest and then returned to her bed. She didn't need to open it to remember the words.

Dear Mom and Dad,

Writing this note is the hardest thing I've ever done, but you must know by now that I'm gone. I left because I'm pregnant. Kevin Slater and I have decided to start our own life for ourselves and our baby in California. Don't try to talk me into coming back because that's not going to happen. Don't worry about me, I'll be fine. Kevin is going to take care of everything.

Denise

She'd read the words over and over again during the weeks after Denise had left, and thinking about them again Charlotte realized Denise was right. Denise never did return to the farm. She couldn't imagine that happening with Sam. Charlotte didn't want to think about him not rumbling down the stairs like a freight train, or emptying her cookie jar in one swoop of his man-sized hand, or sauntering up to the front porch with his skateboard tucked under his arm.

She pressed Denise's letter to her chest and prayed for her daughter's son. She prayed that he wasn't gone for good. Prayed that unlike his mom, he would return to the farm.

Dear Lord, please let us find him. Please keep him safe. Please let Sam know how much we love him.

Charlotte sat there, rocking back and forth as she prayed, unaware of time passing. It could have been five minutes later or fifty when she heard the sound of Pete and Bob heading out to do chores, and Emily's and Christopher's voices coming from the living room. By the serious tone in their voices Charlotte knew her grandchildren were talking about Sam. She opened her bedroom door just a fraction more, hoping they didn't notice her eavesdropping.

"I think Sam went to Seattle—to find our dad."

"Seattle? Is that where Dad is?"

"It's where he went after he left. He told Mom he was going to find work so he could take care of us, but for some reason Mom never wanted to go up there."

"Do you think he found a job?"

"Well, probably. Maybe at a ball park. He would take Sam and me to watch the Padres when we were little, and I'd get to ride on his shoulders. He'd watch the games and tell us everything that was happening. I always thought he'd do a good job as one of the announcers on TV."

"Did I go?"

"No, you weren't born yet—or at least I don't think you were."

"Was Dad nice?"

The simple question caused Charlotte's heart to tie up in a knot.

"Most of the time. He'd give me horse rides on his leg, and he did the best Cookie Monster impersonation ever. I don't remember much, but I do remember when he and Mom used to fight . . ." Emily's voice trailed off, and Charlotte wondered what she was thinking about.

Poor thing, having to go through so much at such a young age.

"If Sam does find him, maybe our dad would take me to a ball park too." Christopher's voice was wistful.

"Yeah, maybe. I'm hungry. Want some cereal?"

After that she could hear the sounds of them in the kitchen, and she returned to her spot on the bed. It was interesting hearing Emily's memories. In fact, it made Charlotte realize that Kevin Slater hadn't always been the enemy. For a while he'd tried his best to take care of his family.

It also made her realize that if Emily had some good memories, Sam no doubt had more. As the oldest, he'd spent the most years with his father. And if Emily was right, and Sam had gone to find him, it was most likely those good memories that urged Sam on.

Knowing that gave Charlotte more to pray about. Not only for Sam, but for the man whom Denise had once loved. The father of Charlotte's grandchildren.

SAM GLANCED OVER his shoulder and noticed the sun's new rays could hardly be seen through the clouds. He shivered on the plastic bus seat and zipped his sweatshirt all the way to the top, wishing he'd brought his new jacket that hung in his closet.

He could feel the cold seeping through the bus windows, and it made his ribs ache even more. All that he could see out was white, white snow drifting down. So much snow he didn't know how the bus driver could see to stay on the road. The only thing he was glad for was that he wasn't driving in it. He hated leaving his car, but seeing how the storm was building made him wonder if he would have made it.

Could have ended up in a ditch somewhere, frozen. At least if the bus got stuck he wouldn't be alone.

Next to him an older woman slept with her head tilted back and her mouth open. She snored slightly, quieter than his grandfather's snores, which often shook the floorboards.

Sam quickly pushed those thoughts out of his mind. He didn't need to think about his warm bed or Grandpa. He didn't need to think about what his grandma was making for dinner, or if Christopher or Emily had started asking about him yet. All Sam needed was to think of his mission— and the future that waited at the end of the bus ride.

He pulled his cell phone out of his pocket and looked at it, refusing to turn it on. If he did he was sure that they could track him. Sam had seen that on television, where a girl got kidnapped in the woods and they were able to find her because of her phone. He wasn't sure if that could really happen, but he didn't want to take any chances. More than that, he was sure if he turned it on there would be a message from Grandma. That's the last thing he needed. He didn't want to think about her or how worried she'd be when she found out. He pushed all thoughts of that out of his mind.

The bus was surprisingly full, yet Sam couldn't sleep, and he didn't spend much time contemplating the people around him. His mind was too busy considering how his life could change in the next day or two.

My father is at the end of this bus ride. I'll get to see him. And then, when he finds out what happened to Mom, he'll want us all to come live with him. Then we can get out of stupid Nebraska. Colorado's better than that. Bigger. More in the twenty-first century.

Sam leaned his head back against the headrest. It smelled like sweat and body odor. He closed his eyes and tried to recall his father's face. He remembered a lot of what they used to do, but he had a hard time picturing what he looked like. The only images Sam had were the frozen ones from the photographs in his baby book. His mom had gotten rid of the other ones. Maybe she tore them up or burned them after his dad had left. Not that it mattered. He'd see his dad again soon.

The bus grinded into a new gear as it chugged up a slippery hill. Sam found himself praying that it would make it to the top of the hill, and to Golden. But when Sam realized what he was doing, he stopped. He was sure that if his grandparents figured out he'd left, they were most likely saying their own prayers. Prayers for his return to Nebraska.

He didn't want to return. Or to be stuck somewhere in the middle. It was bad enough that, because of the weather, the bus that was supposed to arrive at the gas station on Saturday night hadn't got there until Sunday morning. He had spent his first night of freedom chatting with a stranger about people he didn't know and things he couldn't care less about.

And then even after the bus had come and they were on their way, Sam had heard some of the other passengers say the trip might be canceled. He dreaded being abandoned in the middle of nowhere. After having to purchase an unexpected bus ticket, he didn't have much cash left. And no Plan B. Or would that be Plan C?

During the first hour of the bus ride, he'd felt bad leaving Emily and Christopher behind. Ever since his mom's death he had wanted to protect them. But Sam knew that if he'd told either of his siblings about his plan they'd never be able to keep a secret. Christopher wouldn't last ten minutes without spilling the news, and Emily would share with Ashley, and Ashley would tell her mother. And within a day the whole town would know.

It was better this way. He'd been thinking about it for a while, and he knew the longer he waited the harder it would be for his brother and sister when it came to time to leave.

I need to do this alone. It's now or never.

The bus lumbered on, and Sam wished he knew just how far they'd gone and how far they had to go. Even the highway signs were covered with the snow that had blown against them and stuck.

He glanced at his watch again and knew it could be as little as a few hours now until he arrived. Just a few hours until he found his father. Just a few hours until his life would change forever.

Chapter Nineteen

Charlotte had just entered the kitchen when Pete hurried inside with a frosting of snow on his ball cap. She'd expected Bob to be with him.

"Is your dad still in the barn?" she asked.

"No. When I headed out to do the chores he took off. Said he was going to Harding to look for Sam. He wanted to be there by the time the bus station opened at eight o'clock. He wanted to check to see if the ticket guy had seen Sam. He also wanted to drive around to see if he could spot Sam's car."

"He went alone?" Charlotte pressed her hand to her forehead. "How come he didn't come get me?" She walked to the window and looked to where Bob always parked his truck, as if trying to confirm Pete's words.

Charlotte turned to her youngest son. "Do you know if he ate something? If he checked his blood sugar before he left?"

Pete shrugged. "I don't know, Mom. I didn't think to ask. He just told me he was leaving, and then he was gone."

"And what am I supposed to do while he's gone?"

Pete rubbed his stomach. "How 'bout make me breakfast?"

"Is that all you can think about, at a time like this?" Charlotte knew she shouldn't be taking her anxiety out on Pete, but she didn't have the strength to stop herself.

"Well—" Pete looked at the floor. "Think of it this way. If Dad finds Sam, you'll want to have some food around here to feed him, won't you?"

Charlotte didn't want to argue. At least making breakfast would keep her mind off of things.

"Fine, I'll make you some pancakes," she said, getting out the flour and eggs for the batter. "But only if you promise to run upstairs and take a shower. You smell like the barn. I don't think we'll be going to church today, but maybe later you can run me into town to talk with Pastor Evans. He's most likely heard through the grapevine what's going on, but I'd like him to pray for us."

Pete nodded and then trudged upstairs the same way he did when he was six and didn't want to take a bath.

Christopher wandered in from the living room. "Can I help you make pancakes?" he asked, sidling up to her.

"Sure, do you want to stir the batter?"

Christopher nodded.

"Okay, mix this really well while I get out the syrup from the fridge that Sam—" The words caught in her throat. "That Sam made a few days ago."

By the time Charlotte returned with the syrup, there seemed to be more pancake batter on the counter—and her pile of bills—than in the bowl.

"Oh, Christopher," Charlotte muttered.

"What, Grandma?" He gazed up at her with wide eyes.

"Oh, nothing." She grabbed the wet washcloth from the

sink and began wiping down the counter. "Hey, why don't you run upstairs and get dressed while I finish these?"

"Okay." He scurried away as if it were any other day. Sam's empty spot at the table and Bob's missing truck outside the window made it clear that it wasn't.

She tried to wipe the batter off the bills as best she could, and then a new thought stirred. She remembered that charge on the credit card. Could Sam have done it? Maybe it was a clue to finding him.

Pushing the bowl of pancake batter to the side, Charlotte dug through the mail, thankful she hadn't yet filed the bills. There, near the bottom she found the statement.

She looked at it again. There was a set of initials followed by an Internet order number.

"Emily," Charlotte called.

"Yeah?" Emily yawned and stretched from her place on the couch.

"I need you to help me with something on the computer. It might have to do with Sam."

"Okay." Emily jumped to her feet, and within a few minutes they were logged on the computer.

"This looks like something off the Internet, like someone bought something with my credit card." Charlotte showed Emily the bill.

"SPS, yeah, it looks like a business or something."

Emily clicked around for a few minutes, and then a smile spread on her face. "This is it. I found the Web site. It's—"

"SPS, Speedy People Search," Charlotte interrupted. "Sam was trying to find your father."

"Or, mostly likely found him." Emily's eyes widened. She reached her hand for the bill. "Can I see that?"

Charlotte handed it over.

"Yes, this is the order code. Which means Sam had to pay to get information. Maybe if I punch it in, we can see what Sam bought.

Emily typed the number into the search field. A small box popped on the screen.

"Oh rats," Emily mumbled. "It's asking for a password."

"Do you know it?"

"Sam's password? Are you kidding? He'd never tell me. I'll have to try to guess."

"Can you?"

"Well, let's see. Growing up, Mom gave us a password that we'd use to know who to trust. For example, if one of her friends was going to pick us up they had to know it."

"So, maybe that's the one he used?"

"Well, we had a few. Mom changed them every so often."

Emily started typing.

"Okay, not *purple panda*. Not *space goose*."

She typed a few more ideas, and stopped to think. Then she filled the search field one more time. "That's it! She jumped to her feet. *"Fuzzy bunny!"*

Charlotte's mouth dropped open as the page refreshed. Sure enough, there was a search for Kevin Slater.

Emily scrolled down the page. "Wow, Dad has lived a lot of places."

"Washington State, Arizona, Oregon . . . But what's most important is the last one."

Emily scrolled up to the top. "Golden, Colorado. How far is that?"

"I'm not sure. We'll have to ask Grandpa, but I think it can't be more than ten hours away, maybe eight."

Emily stared at the address on the screen.

"Do you think Sam drove there? In his car?"

Charlotte glanced out the window at the dark sky that promised more snow to come. "I sure hope not." She took Emily's hand in hers. "But at least we know which direction to look. Honey, you're awesome. This is a huge help."

"Uncle Pete, Uncle Pete!" Emily raced to the stairs. "Grandma and I think we know where Sam is. He's gone to Colorado to find our dad! We can search for him now!"

Charlotte stayed fixed in the computer chair and stared at the screen. It was hard to believe that Sam had figured out where his father was. Even stranger that he was on his way to find him.

At least we know where to look now. Charlotte tried to figure out how to get ahold of Bob. She needed to talk to him. To tell him what they found.

Realizing that she'd found that "one little clue" that led to the answer, she rose and called Deputy Johnson, who agreed that they'd most likely found Sam's destination. He said he would notify all the small towns along the highway between Bedford and Golden and he would ask Golden police for help too.

Hearing this made Charlotte feel better. Surely with everyone looking along that path they'd discover something soon.

Most of all, she needed a plan for how they were going to get to Golden.

As she was thinking through the possibilities, Pete entered the kitchen, his hair still wet from his shower. "Is it true? Did you find out where Sam is going?"

"I think so. We think he might be in Golden, Colorado, or headed there."

"Did he drive there?" Worry filled Pete's eyes.

"We really don't know." She glanced away.

An hour passed, and Charlotte did anything and every-thing to keep her mind occupied and her hands busy. She was busy folding her third load of laundry when the tele-phone's ringing caused her heart to pound.

"Oh, I hope that's Bob," she mumbled to herself.

She hurried to the phone and answered it.

"Mrs. Stevenson, this is Deputy Johnson."

"Yes, deputy, do you have any news?"

"We found Sam's car. It's in a town a few hours west of Bedford. We talked to a gas station attendant there, who said a young man matching Sam's description got a flat tire and stopped at his station. He said the fellow said some-thing about heading to Denver, and hopped on a bus headed that way."

"Oh, finally some good news," Charlotte sighed.

"It's a start. I don't want to tell you what to do, but my advice . . ." The deputy started and then paused.

Charlotte could hear the sound of muffled voices from Deputy Johnson's radio, making it hard to hear. "My advice," he continued, "is that you try to get to Golden as soon as possible. The more time that passes, the harder it is to find these kids. It's hard to say where Sam will end up. We'll notify the Golden police."

"I agree." Charlotte turned to Pete, her eyes meeting his. "We'll do whatever it takes to bring him home."

The minutes seemed to drag on as Charlotte waited for the phone to ring again. She wanted to call Anna and fill her in, but didn't want Bob or the sheriff's office to get a busy signal if they called. As she waited, Charlotte heard Pete talking on a phone in the other room and she assumed it was Emily's cell phone. She couldn't make out his words, but from his serious tone she guessed he was talking to someone about Sam.

When the phone finally did ring, it was Bob on the other line. "Charlotte, I'm calling from a payphone at the truck stop. Sam's not in Harding."

"I know, Bob. We've discovered where he is headed. Deputy Johnson found his car and talked to someone who saw Sam. More than that, we found the address of Kevin Slater—in Golden, Colorado. That's where Sam's going. Emily found information about their father on the Internet."

"Does his father know he's coming?"

"We don't know yet. Pete's checking on that. I never thought that Sam might have been in contact with Kevin. Maybe Sam called his father before he left. Actually, that makes me feel better, thinking he didn't stay the night alone in an unfamiliar place."

Charlotte felt a hand on her shoulder and turned. "Oh, wait just a minute, Bob."

"Sorry, Mom. I used Emily's phone to call information in Golden. There is no number listed for Kevin Slater. The phone company searched all their records and they haven't had a phone number for him for at least a year. I doubt Sam got ahold of him."

"Oh no. That means Sam most likely went there without his father even knowing he was coming," Charlotte mumbled.

"If Kevin Slater is even still around . . ." Pete added.

"Charlotte?" It was Bob's voice in her ear. "Pack some bags. We'll leave as soon as I get home. We've got to get there." There was urgency in his voice. "We have to find Sam."

Over the next hour Charlotte packed the best she could. It was hard not knowing how long they'd be gone and just what they'd need. She called Hannah to tell her what was going on. Hannah insisted they stop by on the way out of town. Even though everything inside her told her she needed to get on the road to find Sam, she agreed to stop by for just a second.

Pete volunteered to call Bill and Anna. Five minutes after Bob arrived home they pulled into the driveway.

Charlotte watched as they carried two duffle bags from the car.

"Moving in?" Bob joked as he held the door open for Bill.

"Well, actually, we didn't know how long you'd be gone, and we thought it would be easier to stay here."

"What do you mean, stay here?" Bob squared his shoulders.

"You know, to help with Emily and Christopher while you drive to Golden," Anna explained.

"Where are the girls?" Charlotte asked.

Anna slid off her coat and hung it on one of the hooks by the door.

"My mother's at our house. I thought it would be better that they don't get caught up in the drama."

"But there's no need for you two to stay here. Pete will take care of Emily and Christopher." Bob glanced at his youngest son.

"Pete?" Bill's eyes widened in surprise.

"Bill, please . . ." Charlotte put her hand on her older son's shoulder. "Pete's great with the kids, and you don't realize that he's pretty much running the farm." She glanced over at Bob, hoping her words didn't sound disrespectful.

Instead of bristling, Bob nodded. "Exactly. Which is why Pete's going to be in charge while we're gone. You're welcome to visit, of course, but there's really no need to stay."

Bob turned to her. "Ready, Charlotte?"

She nodded and moved to get her coat, ignoring the shocked looks on Bill and Anna's faces, and the slightest smile on Pete's.

"Well." Pete stepped forward. "Have a safe trip. Let us know when you get there."

"Of course." She offered Pete a big hug, then glanced at Christopher and Emily. "You better believe I'll let you all know when we hear something. Hannah's going to let us borrow her cell phone so I'll call if . . . I mean *when* . . . we find Sam."

Emily and Christopher rushed forward and wrapped their arms around her, holding tight. Half of her wanted to get on the road, and half of her didn't want them to let go.

She glanced at Bob and he nodded, understanding. "I'll be waiting in the truck when you're ready. Pete, Bill, Anna—" Then with quickened steps Bob hurried outside. His jaw was set with determination.

We'll do it, she told herself. *With God's help we'll find Sam.*

Chapter Twenty

Charlotte climbed into the truck and waved to the cluster of faces in the kitchen window. "Keep them safe, Lord," she whispered.

As the truck rolled out of the driveway, her gaze took in the white, frozen yard, and in her mind's eye she tried to picture what it would look like in a few months—giant sunflowers and purple dahlias. Green grass. Birds. Now everything was dirty white. Even the sky looked the gray murky color of dishwater.

She shivered, noticing how the bare arms of the cottonwood stretched into the sky, as if attempting to reach the smallest ray of sunlight. Everything around her seemed frozen, dead. Yet her mind was alive, active with questions. *How could they ever find Sam? What was Kevin Slater doing? How will he respond to his son? Did Sam expect to stay with him?*

She had to admit the idea of Kevin taking in Sam scared her. Less than a year ago she had a hard time imagining the kids fitting into the farm. Now, she couldn't imagine the farm without them. Without Sam.

Toby barked nervously as they drove off in the old truck, as if she too realized that everything depended on the next few hours.

"How long does it take to get to Golden?" Charlotte adjusted the heating vent so that the warm air blew on her chilled feet.

"In good weather it's only eight hours. But . . ." Bob gazed up to the sky. "The paper said there is another big storm coming. Let's just hope we beat it."

"I know we're in a hurry, but remember we need to make a quick stop at Hannah's first to pick up her cell phone and some other stuff for the road."

Bob let out a big sigh as he glanced at the sky again.

"I'll run in and run out, Bob. I promise it will be less than five minutes."

Bob glanced at her out of the corner of his eyes. "Does the stuff Hannah has for us have anything to do with food?"

A surprised laugh escaped Charlotte's lips. "I don't know, but I wouldn't be surprised if it did."

Bob turned onto the long driveway leading up to Hannah's house. "If I'm risking not being able to outrun the storm, it had better."

Bob parked the truck, waving to Frank, who was shoveling the snow from in front of his barn door. Charlotte pulled her jacket up to her chin and jumped from the truck, slamming the door behind her.

Her boots crunched in the snow as she hurried up the porch steps. Hannah opened the door even before she knocked and pulled Charlotte inside, and into a warm embrace.

"Oh, Charlotte, I don't know what to say." Hannah's breath was warm on Charlotte's ear. "I'm so sorry you have to go through this again."

Charlotte tried to say something, but she felt the tears building. She pressed her lips together and nodded her head.

"Know that I'll be praying for you, gal. I called the prayer chain at church, and they're all praying too."

Charlotte felt the stone she'd been carrying in her stomach grow heavier. While she was thankful for everyone's prayers, she also knew that along with those prayers would come questions. She also knew that for many of her older friends this scenario was all too familiar.

"Thank you, Hannah. It helps to know that many prayers are going up for Sam."

Hannah stepped back from Charlotte's embrace, but she kept a firm grip on Charlotte's shoulders. "Now listen. Their prayers aren't only for Sam but for you too. I'm sure this is resurrecting all sorts of old feelings and insecurities that should have been done and buried long ago."

"I suppose so." Charlotte wondered how her friend who was younger than she was and who didn't even have kids could be so wise.

"Okay, enough of that." Hannah turned and hurried to the counter, where a picnic basket was waiting. "I've packed a few sandwiches and some cookies. Some dried fruit, and whatever else managed to make it in."

Charlotte took the basket from her, chuckling as its heaviness tugged her arms downward. "We're only driving to Golden. It's not like we're planning to be gone for a month."

"Yes, well, better to be safe than sorry." Hannah waved her hands as if shooing Charlotte out the door. "Hurry now. I don't want to get Bob upset with me." Hannah opened the door. "Call if you hear anything, will ya?"

Charlotte put her hand on the doorknob when Hannah stopped her, grabbing her sleeve.

"Wait! Speaking of calling. I almost forgot the main reason you're here." Hannah grabbed a small plastic bag and handed it to her. "Here's the charger for my cell phone. And here's the phone." Hannah took it out of her purse and slipped it into Charlotte's coat pocket. "It has unlimited minutes, so you can call home and check on the kids whenever you want. Just for a little peace of mind."

"Oh, Hannah, thank you so much. We'll be in touch." Charlotte set the bag on top of the picnic basket and gave her friend a one-armed hug. Then she slipped out the door.

The cold wind blew against her as Charlotte carried the heavy basket to the truck and placed it on the floorboard then climbed in herself.

"Wow, Hannah really loaded you up."

Charlotte nodded and smiled. "Yes, in more ways than one. Food, a cell phone to use, and a few words of encouragement. We're all set."

They drove for a while, passing by Bedford Community Church. Pastor Evans's car was parked in its typical spot and the parking lot was full.

"Is church not out yet?" Charlotte asked. "I wonder if Pastor Evans was especially long-winded today."

Bob tapped his finger on the dashboard. "It's only noon, Charlotte. Church should be going for another thirty minutes, at least."

"It seems later. In fact, it seems like weeks since Sam's been gone, not only one day."

They stopped at the gas station on the edge of town and fueled up. Bob bought extra water for the trip. They rarely got away from the farm—this would have felt like an adventure if it wasn't for the circumstances.

Bob pulled onto the highway and headed west, and for a while Charlotte let her mind reel with thoughts of the reasons for Sam leaving. She watched the other cars on the road but didn't really see them. Even though Hannah had insisted it wasn't her fault, Charlotte couldn't help but letting her mind wander.

Was it us? Did we do something wrong? Did missing his mom trigger it? Or was finding his dad's address enough to start the whole chain of events? And why was he even looking?

The sad thing was Charlotte knew that Sam's story wasn't unusual. In her Bible study group they often prayed for children and grandchildren hurt by divorce, by the abandonment of a parent, by all the other numerous heartaches that came with this generation.

"Things have sure changed. I don't think life is as easy as it used to be," Charlotte said, turning to Bob.

"I know. I would have never thought of running away. I wouldn't know how to survive life outside of Bedford. Still don't. The outside world was just news blaring from the TV. We had innocent fun back when I was Sam's age."

"Yes, I agree. We thought we were so clever, but really we were mostly silly. And we horrified our parents with our pranks," Charlotte said, realizing that this was one of the few times she and Bob had talked one-on-one in weeks.

"How so?" Bob asked.

A smile filled Charlotte's face as she replayed one of her pranks in her mind. "Well, I remember one time some other kids and I were going out to pizza after church. The church pianist jokingly said to save her some. My friend Beverly and I did. We took home a bunch of pizza crusts and wrapped them up in tin foil and then gave them to her on Wednesday. My mother was horrified, of course, but it was fun."

"Oh, that's nothing. Child's play." Bob smirked. "I remember one summer when I went to church camp. A few other guys and I snuck out one night and we stuck the pastor's VW Bug on top of a picnic table."

"You're kidding."

"Nope."

"I've never heard that before."

"Well, once we had kids I didn't want to bring it up. They don't make picnic tables like they used to, you know." Bob chuckled.

It was good to hear him laugh, and it seemed to take some of the tension out of the air too. As they drove they fell into a comfortable silence, lost in their own thoughts.

The truck wound around a curve in the road, and Charlotte braced her hand on the door as she felt the tires of the truck slide. The snow was thick and slushy—white in every direction. Her head ached and her eyes were tired from trying to focus on the road. She could only imagine how Bob must feel.

Sometimes it was impossible to tell where the lanes were. In fact, they hadn't seen another vehicle in over fifteen minutes, and the only hint they were still on the road was the line of reflectors that stretched before them—guiding them to Sam.

After thirty minutes, Bob turned in her direction. "You sleeping?"

Charlotte lifted her head from where it rested on the seatback. "No. Just thinking. Or worrying is more like it."

"I know what you mean."

"What was Sam thinking, Bob? There's a blizzard outside, and he's never even been to Colorado before. Where's he going to stay? What if Kevin isn't there—or worse—won't have anything to do with him?"

"He wouldn't leave his own son out in the cold."

"How do you know that? We haven't seen or heard from the man in almost ten years. He was heartless enough to leave them without ever looking back."

"Maybe he tried."

"What?" Charlotte turned up the heater another notch.

"Kevin. Maybe he tried to contact the kids, and Denise wouldn't allow it. You know how she was when her mind was set on something."

"I can't believe she'd do that. As much as she grew to disagree with Kevin, he still was the father of her children. I think she loved them enough to have dealt with Kevin if he would have given her the chance."

The truck moved on, and Charlotte strained to see ahead, looking for headlights or any other sign of life. It felt so lonely on this road. So slow going. She'd never been lost in the woods, but she got a hint of what it must feel like to want to see someone else out there—some other sign of life.

"I'm so afraid for Sam," Charlotte said, resurrecting their conversation once again. "He could really get lost. Or hurt. There are people out there who could hurt him—if the weather doesn't hurt him more. It doesn't make sense that the police aren't going to search for him. It makes me mad."

"Sam's nearly an adult. This time we found where he was going. This time we're looking for him, but before long he will be grown up, and he'll be making his own choices without our say."

"I don't like the sound of that," Charlotte sighed. "Who knows what type of choices he'll make? No kid should ever have to face losing his mother. For that matter, losing his father too."

"No one has it perfect, Charlotte. If we had it perfect here we wouldn't need a hope in heaven. We wouldn't need God."

Charlotte knew she was tired, she felt herself on edge, and even though she told herself that conversations like this were best held when one was at least halfway rested and not so worried, her mouth kept moving. Just as the snow kept falling out the window.

"I don't want perfection. Just a few breaks. It's not fair that some people have to go through so much loss. Like Sam—"

"And like you?" Bob glanced in her direction. "Or me, for that matter? We've already had to deal with this once—losing Denise. Having her run away. There's enough pain and questions in that for a lifetime. Makes me think of what we're doing wrong."

"We're good parents, Bob. And good grandparents too. Or at least we try to be."

"Yeah, but you have to admit that everyone knows a girl goes looking for love because she hasn't found it at home." Bob tapped his thumbs on the steering wheel as he spoke, as if trying to distract himself from the emotions building. "Maybe I should have given her more hugs. Spent more time with her. Not spent so much time in the fields—"

Charlotte wanted to tell Bob that what he was saying didn't make any sense, but in a way she agreed. She'd thought about that too—although she'd never wanted to admit it. Bob had a hard time knowing what to do with the younger kids. And sometimes she knew Bob used heading out to the fields as an escape. It was easier thinking about soil and seeds, rain, and crop rotation, than how to discipline or interact with the kids.

"I left too much on you," Bob added. "Forced you to try to manage too much. Maybe if I would have been more involved, Denise wouldn't have got involved with Kevin."

"You don't think I discouraged her enough?" Charlotte

leaned up in the seat. "You make it sound like I pushed her into his arms."

"Well, no, but when you learned she was sneaking around to see him, you should have got me more involved."

"Bob Stevenson." Charlotte felt hot anger building up in her. She reached over and flipped the heater down. "After all this time—" She felt her words catch in her throat. "I finally know the truth. You think it's my fault that Denise got pregnant and ran away."

"Now, Char, I never said that." The tires of the truck slid slightly again, and Bob decreased his speed. They were moving barely forty-five miles an hour, but the racing of Charlotte's blood made up for it.

"You just did."

"You didn't argue with me when I talked about not being there for Denise."

"So what you're saying," Charlotte spouted, "is all these years we both blamed each other for what Denise chose?"

Bob didn't say anything, and Charlotte realized he was acknowledging there was some truth to her words. She had blamed Bob's absence, in part. And looking back, she could see why Bob had thought she wasn't strict enough with Denise.

"I could have stopped it." Bob's voice had a haunting sound to it, and for a minute Charlotte wasn't sure if she'd actually heard him speak or had just imagined it.

She turned in her seat to face him. "What do you mean?"

Bob didn't talk for a minute, and then finally he cleared his throat. "A few weeks before Denise ran away, I had a dream. She was five again, just a little girl with blonde pigtails, and she got lost in the cornfield. I knew she was out there, but I couldn't find her. I just kept running and running. I heard her voice, but I couldn't find her."

Even in the dim light Charlotte could see Bob's eyes tearing up.

"You never told me that."

"Yeah, maybe there were ways I blamed you, but I blamed myself more. It was as if God had given me a vision to act on. But I ignored it until it was too late."

Charlotte saw a green road sign ahead and she hoped it would give them a record of how many miles they had left to go. But the closer they got she discovered that the snow had stuck to it—blown against it by the wind, and the white letters couldn't be read. She hated not knowing where they were or how far they had to go on this road. Just as she hated not knowing what lay ahead for the kids.

If only God could give them road signs in life to tell them things like, *You're almost through the big curve,* or *There is a rest stop ahead where you can stop and catch your breath for a while.* Or, *Sam will be waiting at the end of this journey.*

"I'm not sure what to say about the dream," Charlotte finally answered. "Maybe both of us knew more than we'd like to admit that we were losing Denise—that she was slipping through our fingers. Maybe your subconscious was just dealing with that fact."

She scooted over and placed her head on his shoulder. "The thing is, no matter who we blame, or don't blame, there's no going back. We can never rescue Denise. She's gone. I . . ." Charlotte placed her fingers over her lips, willing herself not to cry. "I wish we could go back, but we can't. Maybe God's giving us a second chance to get it right," Charlotte suggested. "I'll take a do-over if it means we can help Sam."

"Look there." Bob pointed to a sign that said Rest Area. "I think we should get out and stretch our legs for a while."

Charlotte climbed from the truck as soon as Bob stopped, pulling her coat tighter around her as she hurried to the small restroom. Bob walked by her side.

"We're going to keep going, right?" she asked.

"Yes, just a short break and then we're going to keep going." Bob reached down and gave her hand a squeeze.

"We have to find Sam," she said, more to herself than to Bob. "He's out there somewhere. And with God's help we can still find him."

Bob walked to the left toward the men's bathroom and she moved to the right. She pushed opened the door, thankful it was warm and clean. Last time they hadn't rushed after Denise. This time they were doing it differently. Last time they'd blamed each other. This time they were pulling together.

No matter how hard it was, maybe they were getting a second shot at doing things right. They were going to do whatever it took to find Sam. It made Charlotte feel better just knowing that. They were in this together, and finding their grandson might heal some of the old wounds they'd ignored over the last eighteen years.

SAM'S HEAD ROCKED against the window of the bus. He'd given up trying to sleep hours ago, and instead began counting the small white poles with reflectors that were spaced evenly along the highway. It amazed him how much he'd come to appreciate those stupid reflectors. Seeing them meant the snow had let up, and that was a good thing. It meant he'd make it to Colorado after all.

His stomach growled, and he pulled a chip bag from his backpack. There were only a few crumbs left in the bottom of the bag, and he lifted it and shook the last of them into his mouth. Then he took the last swig from his bottle of lukewarm water. *So much for dinner . . .*

The fact was, he hadn't eaten much in the last two days.

What was supposed to be a six-hour bus trip from where he'd broken down had dragged out to over twelve hours already, and who knew how much farther they had to go. The storm had slowed them down, in addition to the driver's frequent stops to check on the road. Unfortunately, there hadn't been many stops for food.

If he'd had his car he could have stopped for a burger at one of the few small towns that dotted the route. In the past few weeks, after he'd found his dad's name, he'd thought about waiting until summer—or at least spring—so he could drive safely, but he hadn't wanted to risk it. Once Sam found his dad's whereabouts, he knew he needed to act fast. It was clear from the long list of his dad's previous addresses that he didn't stay in one place long. Waiting risked the possibility of losing his chance, and Sam didn't want that. He'd already lost too much.

561. 562. Counting reflectors was boring, but at least counting was easier than feeling guilty over the fact that he'd left. Easier than questioning what waited ahead. Deep in Sam's gut, hope mixed with fear. His stomach ached from the mixing of the two, and from lack of food.

As the reflectors clicked by, his hunger mounted until all his thoughts centered on one thing—an intense longing for a piece of his grandma's caramel apple pie. As if that would solve all his problems.

"Stop it. Get it out of your head," Sam mumbled to himself.

"You talking to me?" It was the older woman seated next to him. She had woken up without Sam noticing.

"No, I was—just talking to myself." Sam shyly met her gaze.

"Oh my, young people seem to do that a lot." The old woman brushed back a strand of gray hair that had escaped her wool hat. Her face appeared like a map of wrinkles, yet she looked at him with a soft smile. "My great-grandson talks to himself all the time. Quotes from movies and television and things like that. He wants to be a writer for movies, you know. He's gone to Hollywood, and I haven't heard from him in over a year. I suppose these days life's too busy to drop a note in the mail or to pick up the phone."

Thanks for the guilt trip, lady. Sam turned back to the window. "Maybe he'll call when he gets settled. Maybe he's just trying to get on his feet first—to do something to make you proud."

"Could be. But doesn't he know I'm proud just because he's him? Nothing he does will change that or make me prouder."

The woman yawned wide, and then she was silent again. After a few minutes Sam glanced back at her and saw she'd drifted back to sleep.

The woman's words replayed in his mind. Were his grandparents proud of him just for who he was? Sometimes he believed it, but not always. Grandpa always wanted him to be more like him—a happy farmer. And Grandma, well, Sam supposed she wanted him to be less like Pete and more like Bill, the educated, scholarly one. He thought of something else the woman said.

Life's too busy, I suppose, to drop a note in the mail.

He thought about that for a while. Thought about the gift given to him by his grandma. He'd been scared at first to read the letter from his mom. Mostly because he didn't want to think about her. Every time he did that he wanted to cry, and he hated feeling weak like that.

He also knew that reading the letter from her would make him think about what he was doing to his grandparents. Even though she'd also run away, he knew she would have done things differently if she could. She had mentioned that—how running from your problems wasn't the best answer. His mom had also talked over the years about the pain each person's actions can cause others. She'd told him and his brother and sister about the importance of being truthful and honest. And since in the last day Sam had lied, stolen money, and abandoned those who cared for him most, he knew his mom would be shaking her finger at him over his actions. Or more likely, shaking her finger and pointing him back home. She wouldn't have liked the idea of him finding his dad. Not that it mattered now. She was gone, and he was here, and this was Sam's only hope of getting out of Nebraska.

"My mom made up for what she did." Sam mumbled, glancing at the old woman to make sure she didn't hear him. "She left and then made things right later."

What was that saying he'd heard before? *Better to beg for forgiveness than ask for permission . . .*

Sam liked that quote, and he set his jaw. Then he opened his backpack, pulled out the Bible, and slipped out the letter. Better to just get it over with. It was just a letter, after all.

Yet his heartbeat quickened when he noticed his mother's handwriting. And even before he read the first word, tears lined the lower rims of his eyes.

Dear Mom,

Even though you already know a little about your grandson from our talk on the phone, I wanted to tell you a little more about Sam, my son. Even saying those words overwhelms me. I can't believe I'm a mom. I think I gave away my heart to this kid, and I have no hopes of getting it back.

Enclosed are two photos. The first was taken at the hospital. The second at La Jolla Shores, our favorite beach. Isn't Sam cute in his little sun hat?

I have to tell you, Sam is a great baby. He loves to be hugged and held, especially snuggled close to my chest where he can hear my heartbeat. Sam's name means "God heard," and even though Kevin wanted our son named after him, I insisted on this name. You see, Mom, even though you think I abandoned my faith, that's not true. And even though I know there are still problems between me and my family—especially with Dad—my son is a great gift. He's something good that has come out of a lot of mistakes. I think God heard the prayers that have gone up for me and Sam. That's why I chose this name.

I have big dreams for my boy. For a safe, happy place where he can grow up. For a family that will love him despite his mistakes. To enjoy the beauty of nature and a community that will guide him as he grows.

Pray for me, Mom—that Kevin and I can find something like that for him. A happy place like I had growing up in Nebraska. And pray that I can be a good mom. I'm not sure if I can pray for myself, but I know God hears your prayers for me and Sam.

Okay, I better go. It's time for his feeding. Tell everyone I said hi and that I'm okay—as good as good can be.

Love, Denise

P.S. Sam sends all his love to Nebraska too!

Sam closed the letter and held it firmly in his hands. His throat felt tight and thick and he wished he had more water. He didn't know what he expected, but it wasn't that. He tried to remember if his mom ever told him why she'd picked his name. Or the fact that she didn't feel like she could pray. Over the years, they prayed at dinner when they remembered and sometimes they prayed before bed. But is that the type of praying his mom was talking about? The simple habits that she'd carried with her from her childhood? Or was she talking about something more?

His mom believed God heard his grandparents' prayers. Were they praying now? Praying to find him? And, more importantly, would God answer them? He hoped not. At least until he found his dad.

He read the letter again, rereading about what his mother wished for him. A safe, happy place. A family that loved him. Nature. Community.

Sounds like Nebraska, what I'm leaving behind . . . Maybe his mom wanted him to have what she'd experienced growing up. The only problem was he had to lose her to get it. Personally, he didn't think it was a fair trade. And, if Sam had his way, he hoped to find those things in a different place.

With my dad.

Sam put the letter back into the Bible and stuck them both in his backpack. Then he pulled out his iPod and put the ear buds into his ears. He turned on his favorite rock band and turned the volume up loud. He guessed even the old lady sitting next to him would be able to hear the music, but he didn't care. Sam needed it loud. He needed it to drown out the questions that kept running through his head.

Chapter
Twenty-One

The sun was just beginning to set when Emily heard the knock at the door and hurried to it. She opened it to find Miss Simons there with her hands holding her coat's hood around her face, shivering in the cold.

"Miss Simons! Come on in." Emily stepped aside, and Dana did as she was told.

Emily slammed the door shut, locking it so that the wind wouldn't blow it open.

"Hey there, Emily. I heard from Melody Givens what was happening and I thought I'd offer to help." Dana pushed off her hood and ran her fingers through her hair.

"Dana!" Pete's voice came from the living room. He was wearing a bath towel tied over his shoulders as a cape. Christopher was wearing the same and they both had sheepish grins on their faces. "We were, uh, just playing Superhero checkers."

Emily glanced at the checkerboard on the living room floor. "Yeah, and they're not joking. For the last hour, I've been hearing things like, "I'll use my ability to jump tall buildings—and to jump your red checker with a single bound." Emily sighed. "I'm so glad you're here. I need someone in touch with reality. These guys are crazy, Uncle Pete especially."

Dana didn't respond at first, but when Emily glanced up she saw a tenderness toward Pete she hadn't expected.

"Yeah, he's completely nuts all right," Dana said with a smile, brushing her dark hair back from her face. Then she turned to the kitchen.

"I noticed Bill and Anna's car wasn't here. I expected them to—you know—be around at a time like this."

"Nah, Grandpa said that Uncle Pete could handle everything. They came and left. I think they've called a few times, but I don't expect them to come over until tomorrow."

Dana placed her hands on her hips. "Well, are you hungry? I could whip something up."

Emily nodded. "Yeah. I had cereal for breakfast and a peanut butter and jelly sandwich for lunch. I could use some real food."

"What do you think about helping me make some spaghetti? When I was your age my grandma taught me her secret recipe, and I haven't made it for Pete yet."

She hurried over to the cupboard and took out the tall stock pan, filling it with water from the faucet.

"Sam really liked spaghetti," Emily mumbled to herself.

She didn't want to tell Dana, but the truth was she hadn't eaten much because her stomach hurt and she couldn't imagine sitting down to enjoy a meal. How could anyone eat during a time like this? Sam was out there somewhere— alone. He could be in trouble.

Emily moved to the dining room and sat in the kitchen chair, willing herself not to throw up. Now Grandpa and

Grandma were out there too. She knew they were old. She also knew the roads were dangerous. What if something happened to them before they found Sam? What if she lost *three* more members of her family?

"Need help with that?" Pete removed his cape and hurried into the kitchen, ready to become a real hero.

"Can I help too?" Christopher asked, hurrying in, sidling up to Pete. From Emily's point of view they looked like the perfect little family—a mom, dad, and son in the kitchen. And as Emily watched Dana she could tell that Pete's girlfriend was thinking the same thing too.

Dana was actually humming as she took a jar of tomatoes from the pantry. Then Dana paused before Pete. "Do you think you can open these for me?"

"Sure, not a problem." Pete gently took the jar from her hands.

"Oh, Mom's tomatoes are best," Pete said. "You're gonna love them." He opened the jar and handed it back. "You know, I'm really excited about spring because I'm going to double the size of the garden. With our bigger family now, we need more produce. I can't wait to get on my tractor and get to work, digging up the soil."

Pete ruffled Christopher's head. "You wanna help me plant this year, buddy?"

"Can I, Uncle Pete?" Christopher's eyes widened.

Emily placed her fingertips on her temples, realizing her head was starting to hurt. She wanted to call Grandma and talk to her—to check to make sure everything was okay, but didn't want to bother her.

Dana grabbed half of an onion and a clove of garlic out

of the refrigerator. Pete pulled out the chopping block and a knife. Emily was sure this was one of the only times she'd ever seen him help in the kitchen. *So much for Dana needing my help.* Still her mind wasn't too concerned with that. Her heartbeat actually quickened in her chest as she thought about calling Grandma.

"Uncle Pete?" Emily clapped her hands together. "Can we call Grandma? Remember, Miss Hannah stopped by to give us the number of the cell she loaned her."

"Sure, just don't stay on too long," Pete said. "I don't want to use up all Hannah's minutes. I hear that costs a fortune. Actually, let me call and then I'll pass it over to you."

"The cost of minutes isn't too bad . . . depending on Hannah's plan," Dana assured him.

Pete picked up the house phone and dialed the number. He sat there, waiting for someone to pick up, but Emily could tell it went to voice mail.

"Sorry, guys. It must be out of range." Pete shrugged then hung up the phone. "We'll try again later."

Emily felt her stomach turn, and she imagined her grandfather's truck stuck in a ditch. She felt herself growing cold, and then the voices in the room started to get fuzzy.

"Emily?" It was Dana's voice. "Are you okay?"

"No, I don't think so." She hurried to the bathroom. "I think I'm going to be sick."

Emily closed the door and leaned against it. Slowly her stomach calmed, and then the tears came.

"God, if you're real and if you're out there, would you please take care of my family?" It was a simple prayer.

She just hoped it was good enough.

CHARLOTTE NOTICED BOB'S KNUCKLES were white as he gripped the steering wheel and gazed into the snow. Charlotte rubbed her eyes. They burned from staring so hard into the stormy night, and she wasn't even the one driving. At least they were together. And at least they were warm. She wished she could do more, but the last thing she wanted was to volunteer to drive in this mess.

"Doing okay?" Charlotte patted her husband's arm.

"Yeah, although I'm a little upset that we can't go faster. I've been driving less than 45 miles per hour for the last two hours. At this rate we'll be lucky to make it to Golden by dawn."

Charlotte studied Bob's tense jaw. He wasn't a patient man. He liked fixing things and solving problems, and she knew the fact that he couldn't fix the weather would only make him crankier as they traveled on.

She tried to think of something to talk about. Something to keep his mind off the weather. They'd talked about Pete and Dana, planting season, and the rising cost of groceries, but she was running out of interesting things to talk about, especially things that didn't involve the kids.

"Oh, great," Bob mumbled under his breath.

"What? What's wrong?" Charlotte sat up straighter in the seat.

"There are flares up ahead. That can't be a good thing."

Bob slowed the truck. They could see a blue sedan stuck nose first into a ditch. And on the other side of the road a car and a truck appeared to have collided. Bob stopped the truck, thumping his palms on the steering wheel. "Of all things. Wonder how long this is going to take."

They didn't have to wait long to hear the answer. A sheriff's deputy moved toward their truck, half walking and half sliding on the ice.

"Sorry, folks. You won't be able to get by for a long while. There's a big mess up there, and all the tow trucks are out on other calls."

"How long do you think we'll have to wait?"

"Wait? I wouldn't recommend that at all." The deputy's radio squawked on his hip, but he ignored it. "We could be dealing with this mess until mornin'. My suggestion is to turn around and head back."

He told them to head back to the small town they had just passed. "They have a nice hotel there. Had to stay there myself on other nights like this. I reckon they'll have a room for you if you hurry."

Bob nodded. "Guess we don't have a choice. Thank you, deputy."

The deputy walked away, taking every step with care. Bob rolled up the window.

"Looks like we're not getting to Golden tonight. Or anytime early in the morning."

Charlotte crossed her arms over her chest. Having the window down had brought in a rush of cold air, but she knew that wasn't the only reason she was shivering. She hated the thought of turning back. Sam was out there in this mess—alone.

With effort, Bob turned the truck around. They found the small town and the hotel. Thankfully, Bob didn't even bat his eye at the price of the room. It needed to be done; they had no choice.

Together they lugged their suitcase and Hannah's picnic

basket into the room. It was sparse and quiet. So different from home. Charlotte wondered if she would be able to sleep. At least she'd have Bob's snoring to make it like home. She smiled to herself at that thought. Charlotte got ready for bed, then she set the alarm for 5:00 AM. Bob watched her and didn't comment. She knew he was just as eager to get on the road—to get to Sam. At least they'd get a little time to rest. Who knew what tomorrow held.

IT WAS NEARLY MIDNIGHT when the bus neared Golden, Colorado. Sam cupped his hands around his eyes and tried to peer out the window, but all he could see was snow and more snow—even deeper than in Nebraska.

He pulled the slip of paper out of his pocket and glanced at the address one more time. Then he slid the address into his Bible next to his mom's letter. He tucked his Bible into his backpack.

Every time he looked at that Bible he couldn't help but think about his grandma. Her smile. Her laugh. The way she looked at him with uncertainty—her brows slightly furrowed—whenever she didn't know how to handle a situation, which was often. He thought about spring on the farm, which was right around the corner. About cinnamon rolls from Mel's Place, and even the church services that had sort of grown on him. And then, trailing all those thoughts came a deep longing for his brother and sister.

The emotion surprised Sam. He'd always considered them pests, or burdens to take care of, or both. But now he knew he'd do anything for them. His shoulders felt tight, and his chest felt empty with missing things back home.

The only thing that helped was knowing that if things went well with his dad he wouldn't have to be apart from Christopher and Emily for long. But what if they wanted to stay in Nebraska? What would he do then?

With a creak of brakes and a loud sigh, the bus stopped. The driver announced their arrival at the Golden, Colorado, bus station, and said the bus would be departing again soon.

The lady next to him gathered her things and exited. Sam knew the time had come. He stood and grabbed his backpack and the additional duffle bag of things he'd brought—clothes, his favorite CDs, and another pair of shoes. As he walked down the aisle of the bus, he tried to picture what it would be like to see his father again. His mind replayed what he was going to say to his dad.

"Hey there, remember me?"

"So, how have you been? Long time no see."

"I have some news. It's about Mom."

"Well, Pops, what would you think of raising three kids?"

The cold wind blew through the bus door, and Sam stepped down into the snow. It was deep and wet, and he wished he had boots on. A chill numbed his body and he trudged forward, wondering where to go and what to do. There were a few others also getting off the bus, but they had people waiting for them.

In a few minutes the bus pulled away, and so did the cars. Sam still stood there, his back against the cold brick of the bus station, trying to shield his body from the cold wind and decide his next step.

What was I thinking?

He knew it was too late to find his dad's place tonight, but where to go until morning was the big question. As he looked around at the line of unfamiliar buildings surrounding him, another deep longing for his grandparents' warm farmhouse caught him by surprise. *Don't wimp out now. You haven't come this far for nothing.*

"Don't think about home, Sam. Just do what you have to do," he mumbled to himself, looking around.

He spotted a hotel down the road, but decided that wasn't an option. He couldn't imagine spending all that money for one night. Instead, he noticed what looked like a twenty-four-hour Laundromat and jogged across the street with the snow squeaking under his sneakers.

He pushed the door open, and saw that the place was empty. It was warm and lighted—a safe place to wait it out. In the back was a vending machine. He thought he'd get something to eat and catch a nap.

The place smelled like Grandma's laundry room and the stacks of folded clothes he found on his bed every other day. With the scent and that memory, the longing for his own bed stirred, but he pushed that out of his mind.

No looking back. Only ahead. Only to the future . . .

Looking around for the safest out-of-the-way place to stretch out, Sam wandered to the back and dropped to the floor. Then, with a large yawn, he leaned against his bag and stuck one arm through the straps of his backpack for safety. Then he pulled his hat lower over his eyes, and with thoughts about tomorrow's meeting filling his mind, he attempted to fall asleep.

"Hey, kid, whatya doing in here?" The sharp words woke Sam just seconds before he felt a firm kick to the bottom of his shoe.

He opened his eyes to find a tall, stocky man looking

down on him. About ten feet away a side door opened to an office.

"This ain't no homeless mission. Get outta here," the man growled.

"But I'm not homeless . . ." It was the first thing that popped into his mind. Sam rubbed his eyes and stood, wondering how long he'd been asleep. "I just needed to warm up."

"Got any place to sleep tonight?" the man asked, folding his arms over his chest.

"No, but—"

The man raised his hands and interrupted Sam's words. "Like I said, I'm not Mother Teresa. If you ain't got no place to go then you *are* homeless. So you need to take your bags and leave my property. I'll give you thirty seconds."

Sam eyed the older man, spotting hardness in his gaze, and knew he didn't want to argue. Jumping to his feet, he hurried out the door into the cold night.

Maybe I can just walk around until morning. Keep my blood circulating. Keep myself warm. He walked a few more blocks, glancing at the street signs and attempting to remember his path. No matter how briskly he walked, he couldn't get warm. By now his sneakers were wet, as were the bottom of his pants legs. His feet felt frozen solid and he thought about a movie he'd watched about a guy who'd got lost in the wilderness and whose frozen toes snapped off like dry twigs. The thought of it made Sam's stomach hurt even more.

Resignation overcame him as Sam realized he needed a hotel room, and would have to use his emergency money. *Make that Grandma's grocery money.*

He had contemplated for two days whether or not he

could take it. He felt horrible stealing from his own flesh and blood, but he finally justified it by telling himself his grandma would want him to have emergency money—which now made no sense because if he thought about it he assumed her first choice would be that both he and the money had stayed put.

Up ahead, Sam spotted a dingy-looking hotel. It looked like it hadn't been renovated for the last fifty years, but the price in the window encouraged him.

He entered the small lobby, noticing the man behind the counter was sleeping.

"Excuse me. I'd like a room." His jaw was quivering from the cold.

"Cash only." The man mumbled, hardly lifting his head.

"Sure, okay." Sam lifted his backpack off his shoulder and noticed the front pocket where he'd stashed Grandma's cash was unzipped—and empty. *What happened? Where did it go?* His stomach clenched in panic. With a dull, sick feeling, he realized he was broke except for the ten bucks he still had in his wallet.

Did the guy at the Laundromat take it? Did it fall out when I was walking? There was no way of knowing now.

"Uh, listen. Someone took my money. Could I just hang out here for a little bit? In the lobby—just for a few hours. I need to find my dad, see?"

"Cash only," the man repeated, waving Sam away.

Sam had no choice but to trudge back into the cold. He retraced his steps, hoping that the cash would show up, but after a few blocks he knew it was pointless. Since he didn't have a phone number for his dad, he couldn't call him. Sam had no idea how to find his house in this huge town.

He pictured calling his grandparents, but to do that would be to admit defeat. If he was old enough to run away, he was old enough to take care of himself.

He wasn't doing a very good job though.

Not knowing what else to do, Sam crossed the street to a small park. *Maybe there's an open restroom or something.* He veered toward a small building, and noticed it looked to be some type of maintenance shed. *Please be unlocked. Please be unlocked!* He turned the knob but it didn't budge. *Dear God, please.* He tried again and this time the door moved. He pushed harder and it swung open.

Sam hurried inside. He flipped on the light just for a second to get his bearings. It had bags of salt for icy sidewalks, a few shovels, and a big machine he guessed was a snow blower. It wasn't heated, but it was warmer than outside, and it protected him from the wind.

Knowing he had to get out of his wet clothes, Sam stripped down and then dressed in all the remaining clothes he brought, layer upon layer.

Then, with an extreme weariness coming over him, Sam curled up in a ball on the concrete floor. His stomach growled, and he couldn't help but think of his warm bed and Grandma's cooking. Heck, he knew even the hens slept more comfortably than he was tonight.

Tomorrow. Sam's chin quivered. *Tomorrow it will all be worth it.*

Chapter
Twenty-Two

Sunrise was about to break when the tinny song from the cell phone stirred Charlotte awake.

Charlotte grabbed it from the nightstand, then she clicked the button to answer it, putting it to her ear.

"Hello?" she croaked, her voice scratchy from sleep.

"Hello? Mom? Hello, are you there?"

"Oh, Pete. Is everything okay?"

"Yes, are you okay? We tried to call you a few times last night but the call didn't go through."

"Yes, we're fine. We had to stop last night because of the weather. But I think we're getting close to Golden—"

"Hold on, Mom, before you fill me in, can you say hello to Emily real quick?"

"Sure. Is everything okay?"

"Yeah, she's okay. She just had a rough night. Here you go."

"Grandma?" Emily's voice quivered.

"Yes, Em. It's us."

"Did you find Sam yet?"

"No, not yet, but we're getting close to Golden."

"Okay." Emily paused. "Are you and Grandpa okay?"

"We sure are. Do you want to talk to your grandfather?" Charlotte glanced at Bob and noticed him rubbing the sleep from his eyes. She also looked at the clock and noticed it was almost 7:00 AM, which meant she'd set the alarm clock wrong.

"No, it's okay." Emily's voice was full of emotion. "Just call me when you find Sam, okay?"

"Sure, sweetheart. We will."

"Mom?" It was Pete's voice again. "I'm back."

"Have you heard anything from Sam? Or has the deputy called you?"

"Deputy Johnson finally called back just a few minutes ago, which is the main reason why I called. I'm not sure what took so long, except there are all kinds of issues that the weather's bringing up—power loss, people stuck in ditches. But, I wanted to tell you that Deputy Johnson notified the police in Golden. Of course, he doesn't know how much they'll be able to do. I'll let you know if I hear anything." Pete sounded so together—so professional. And responsible too.

"Sounds like you've got things under control." Charlotte rose and moved to the window. She pulled back the thick shades and was surprised to find the sun had come up. "Did Bill and Anna stay, after all?" she asked.

"No. They left right after you and Dad did. They didn't seem too happy about it, but they called later to check on things. They said since they were free, they were going to an evening prayer meeting at the church, most likely to pray for their heathen brother, needy parents, and wayward nephew. I haven't heard a peep out of them since."

"Yes, well, we can all use prayer . . ." Charlotte said, trying to calm Pete's frustration. "There's nothing wrong with turning to God, especially during times like this. But maybe you're right. After the episode the other day, I'm afraid they have their doubts."

"Yeah, well, they don't live here. They don't see how things work. They don't know the love and attention you and Dad pour into these kids." He paused as if surprising himself with his words.

Charlotte placed a hand over her heart, not realizing how much she needed her son's words. "Thanks, Pete. That makes me feel better. Let me know if you hear anything."

"Okay, Mom, you do the same."

Charlotte hung up and relayed the information to Bob, including what Pete said about Bill and Anna.

"They are just that way, Char." He reached over and patted her hand. "You know Bill. There's only one right way to do things—his."

"Yeah, well, to tell you the truth, that sounds a little familiar," Charlotte said with a smile. "But maybe they have a point. Maybe we should have considered letting the kids live with them. They're younger. They're more connected in the community. They live in a town, which might have been easier to adjust to." Charlotte rose and pulled her fresh clothes from the suitcase.

"Do you really think that, or are you just letting your mouth rattle off?" Bob smiled. "If you think things have been tough around our place, could you imagine all the rules around Bill's house? I'm certain I've never seen a speck of dust. The kids would have more chores than they have now."

He laughed. "And can you imagine the clothes issue— Anna trying to dress Emily to match Madison and Jennifer? I love those little girls with all my heart, just like I love all my grandkids, but sometimes kids need to be kids, you know?"

Charlotte laughed, trying to imagine it too. She placed her clothes on the bed and then smoothed the covers, even though she knew the maids had to change the sheets. Even though it made no sense, Charlotte couldn't leave the room with the bed unmade.

"Christopher would have really had a hard time," she added as she walked to the bathroom. "Can you picture him bringing his 'treasures' home in Anna's house? The sticks and pinecones and rocks? That kid has quite a collection."

"Maybe Sam would have run away sooner." Bob shrugged. "Maybe we should be commended that he lasted as long as he did. You know how from the beginning he'd threatened to head back to California."

"Yes, you're right." She rubbed her eyes. "So I think we both agree that we've made the best choice for where the kids should be."

Bob nodded. "Yes, I agree."

Charlotte took her shower and dressed. Exiting the bathroom, she found Bob sitting on the bed, flipping through the channels. Hearing her exit, Bob turned to her. "You know what yesterday was?"

"No, what?" Charlotte ran her finger through her damp hair.

"The day I was supposed to take Sam to the snowmobile races."

"Yes, you're right . . ." She approached and sat next to

Bob. She patted his hand and studied his face. His eyes were fixed on some cooking show on cable, but she could tell he wasn't really watching it. Instead, she could see sadness on his face. "Maybe you'll have another chance to go to the races after Sam comes home."

"Yup. Maybe."

Chapter
Twenty-Three

S am woke up with a start and wondered where he was. Sunlight streamed through two high windows, and amazingly the chill he felt during the night was gone. He almost felt warm, and he pulled off his socks and checked his toes. They looked pink, and he wiggled them just to make sure.

His next thought was of his dad. Sam glanced at his watch and was surprised to see it was only 7:00 AM. It was the first time he'd been able to sleep late for months and still he got up early. If he was back in Bedford he'd be heading to school. But he wasn't. When morning roll call was taken, his seat would be empty. It would be all too evident to everyone that he was gone. Soon, the other kids would know about him running away. Were they talking about him? Glad he was gone? Waiting for his safe return? Were his grandparents trying to find him?

"I don't need to be saved," he mumbled as he rose and stood. Then again . . . he looked around at the small space that just happened to be unlocked, and he realized that perhaps some of his grandparents' prayers had already been answered.

Sam straightened his clothes the best he could, wishing he had a mirror and a razor. He hoped he could find a bathroom somewhere to brush his teeth and wash up before he hunted down his father's address. It would be the first time his dad had seen him in ten years. He wanted to look decent.

Sam left the small building, looking around to make sure no one saw him. The park was mostly empty, and the street was too. Only one car passed by. More snow had fallen as he'd slept, and for the most part it looked undisturbed.

He found his way back to the road and noticed he wasn't far from the bus station. *All that walking, and I got back almost to where I started.*

Beyond the bus station he noticed a fast-food joint. He hurried his pace, knowing that food—and a restroom— were close. His stomach growled as he walked through the door. First, he used the facilities, and then he scanned the menu. Pancakes. Grandma made them many mornings— including the day he left—and he couldn't think of anything that sounded better.

He ordered them, and then sat at a table in the corner and took a big bite. "Ugh." He nearly spit it out. "How do people eat this stuff?" he mumbled to himself. The pancakes tasted like Styrofoam. He realized how much things had changed since he'd started living on the farm. Like his taste in food. He remembered that this pancake breakfast used to be his favorite—a real treat when his mom could take him out. Not anymore.

He choked down the pancakes the best he could, then drank the small milk that also tasted like the carton, trying not to think of the fresh cow's milk in Grandma's fridge.

He comforted himself with the thought that he would see his dad soon.

Sam realized he needed to find a map of the area. He walked down the sidewalk with his backpack slung over his shoulder and checked out the businesses he passed, hoping one of them had some type of visitor's information booth. He thought about asking for directions from a cashier or something, but after all the "help" he got last night he didn't know how much help store clerks would be.

"You looking for the youth center?" A woman paused in front of him. She had dark fuzzy hair that stuck out from under a colorful stocking cap; she was walking a large dog on a leash.

"Uh, no. Thanks. Just walking." He kept moving forward, refusing to meet her gaze.

"Do you have a place to stay?"

This caused him to pause. Sam glanced back at her.

"I don't know, but I think I will. I'm here looking for someone." Sam scratched his head.

"Well, if you're looking for the teen center, it's right around the corner and down the street. I have some bunk beds in a back room. It's warm and there's food in the fridge."

Sam opened his mouth to say something but then closed it again. The woman looked nice enough, but then again so did most mass murderers.

The woman nodded as if reading his mind. "Yeah, I wouldn't trust a stranger either. But if I'm guessing correctly you just left home recently but haven't really found what you were looking for."

Sam crossed his arms over his chest. "Listen, lady, I don't mean to be rude, but I'll be okay, really."

She shrugged. "Okay, but if you need a place—later. I've helped a lot of people."

Sam turned, and then he thought of something. He turned back and wasn't surprised that the woman was still standing there. Both she and her dog were looking at Sam with big, brown concerned eyes.

"Uh, I was wondering if you could give me directions. I'm looking for 437 Maple, apartment number nine."

"Maple? Yeah, I know where that is. It's on the other side of town—at least ten miles away. Is that where your friend lives?"

"Yup, my friend."

"Well, I could give you a ride if you'd like. I was just going to get some breakfast. Maybe we should eat first. You hungry?"

Sam had eaten all the Styrofoam pancakes, but they didn't come close to filling him up. "A little."

"Okay, let me call my friend. We were supposed to meet for lunch but I'll reschedule."

Sam nodded and watched as the woman walked a few feet away and then made a call on her cell phone. He could hear her say something about finding a kid who needed help and would have to take a raincheck—as if this type of thing happened every day.

The dog moved to the end of his leash, toward Sam, and the woman released the leash. The dog approached Sam and sat at his feet.

"Hey, fella." Sam leaned over and scratched the dog's ear.

"You're a nice boy." Sam felt a peace come over him, and he didn't realize until then how much he'd hated being alone. And now this woman and her dog were going to help him. The woman ended her call and approached, grabbing the leash again.

"Okay, thanks for waiting. I'm Maggie, by the way." She stretched out her gloved hand and he shook it. "We're heading to that little café right across the street. It has the best food in town."

Sam told her his name and followed her in while the dog waited outside.

"Hi, Maggie, can you believe winter's not letting go?" The short, round waitress led them to a table by the window.

"It will have to soon. Winter doesn't last forever." Maggie chuckled.

Through the window of the small café, Sam could see a sign that read, "Howdy, Folks. Welcome to Golden." He could also see Maggie's dog sitting patiently outside the door. A few people walked up and down the streets, and Sam watched them, wondering if one of them could be his dad. He also questioned if he was doing the right thing. *Wouldn't it be easier to just head across town myself? I could see my dad now. What am I waiting for?*

The restaurant was small inside, with no more than a dozen tables around the room. The scent of coffee and baked treats reminded Sam of Mel's Place. It was warm and inviting, and Sam felt content being here. After what had happened yesterday, he finally felt safe.

Sam felt eagerness over the reunion, but more than that he felt anxiety. Sam didn't want to face another night like last night again. He still didn't know who this woman was, but at least he'd get a meal and a ride.

"Two specials, Judy," Maggie called. "Sam, I assume you like scrambled eggs? And are blueberry pancakes okay?"

"Yeah, uh, sure. Thanks."

Sam's eyes moved back outside, and Maggie turned in her seat to follow his gaze. "Cute town, isn't it? It was founded during the Pike's Peak gold rush. It used to be called Golden City, but, well, it isn't much of a city. Most people just think of it as part of Denver now."

Sam nodded, unsure why she was telling him all this.

The waitress brought Maggie a cup of coffee.

"Thanks, hon," Maggie said, then turned back to Sam.

"So, tell me about the friend you're trying to find. Has he or she lived here long?"

Maggie had an honest, kind face. Round and kind. She wasn't wearing any makeup but she was pretty just like his grandma was pretty. Sam had a strange feeling he could trust her, and he felt his guard coming down.

"My friend, he hasn't been here too long. Less than a year." He looked straight at Maggie. "It's my dad, actually."

"Your dad? That's interesting. What's his name? I know a lot of people around here."

Sam took a sip of his water. "I don't know if you'd know him, especially if he lives on the other side of town. But, uh, his name is Kevin Slater."

"Yeah, you're right, I don't know him. I mostly work with teens. After we eat I'll take you to the youth center and I'll show you around."

"Maybe. I don't know. Maybe I should just try to find my dad."

Maggie shrugged, causing her curly brown hair to

bounce on her shoulders. "Doesn't matter to me. I'll give you a ride; that's no problem. I just thought you'd want to call whoever is back home and let them know you're okay."

Sam nearly choked on the sip of water he was taking. He coughed, and it took everything within him not to spit the water onto the table. "What are you talking about?"

Maggie leaned forward, resting her hands on the table. "Listen, Sam, I've been helping kids like you for many years. From all that stuff you're hauling around you're not just out for an overnight sleepover. From the five o'clock shadow on your jaw it's been a few days since you've showered and shaved—and I can see that look in your eyes. You're worried about the people back home who are missing you—maybe looking for you."

A lump formed in Sam's throat as he thought about his grandparents calling around, frantically asking strangers for help.

"So is it your mom looking for you? An older brother or sister?"

"Grandparents." Sam swallowed hard, especially as he thought about them having to deal with this for a second time. He'd always heard the story of his mom running away, but it hadn't seemed like reality until now.

"I guess I didn't think much about my grandparents before I left." Now he thought about Emily and Christopher too, but he didn't want to talk about them, even though he could tell from the look in the woman's eyes that she knew he was holding back.

"We better pray for them then. When we get our pancakes we'll pray for our food *and* your grandparents."

A few minutes later, a stack of fluffy blueberry pancakes showed up with a side of scrambled eggs. And, as promised, Maggie prayed—for the food, for Grandma and Grandpa, for Sam, and for Kevin Slater. She prayed for them as if she'd known them all her life. She also didn't mind the looks of those sitting nearby who glanced in their direction more than once. Sam knew this because he too was glancing around and looking at Maggie in wonderment at her heartfelt prayers.

Sam took a bite of the pancakes, and he couldn't believe how much they tasted like home, like Nebraska. And as Sam chewed he realized he now considered the two the same. *Nebraska has become like home.*

Maggie too dug into her breakfast with a flourish. They mostly ate in silence, but there was one thing he just had to ask.

"So, Maggie, why did you take time to help me, especially canceling the stuff you were gonna do?"

"I may be missing a gathering of my friends from church, whom I consider my family, but ever since I opened the youth center years ago I have a new idea of what being a believer is all about." Maggie smiled. "I enjoy my friends, but if one of my kids needs to go out to breakfast, to talk, to pray together, well, that comes first. A believer is someone who acts on what she or he knows to be true."

Sam nodded, and it seemed to make sense to him. A lot of the people he knew did things for others, but he'd never really thought of it this way before.

"But enough about me. Tell me about yourself." Maggie took a big bite from her pancakes.

"I don't know." Sam shrugged. "I have a brother and sister. I like to skateboard and play soccer. I kicked for the football team last fall. And I have a car that runs half of the time, but right now it's out of commission."

Maggie took a sip of her coffee and then leaned against the table as if Sam was the most interesting person she'd ever met. "Really? Tell me about that."

So Sam did. He told her about trying out for the football team, and about his recent biff on the skateboard. He told her about getting fired from his job and about leaving his car parked at some gas station on the edge of Nebraska.

"And how long have you been with your grandparents?"

He counted in his head. "Ten months or so."

She nodded and waited like she wanted him to continue.

"We moved in with them. After my mom died."

"And your dad? He hasn't been around for a while, has he?"

Sam lowered his head. "No."

Maggie was quiet, and Sam pushed the rest of his scrambled eggs back and forth on his plate—his appetite completely gone.

"I'm so sorry, Sam."

Sam gulped back his emotion, not wanting to cry in front of this stranger. And when he glanced up he noticed tears in her eyes.

She took a twenty-dollar bill from her wallet and set it on the table. Sam pulled some change from his front pocket and added it too.

"C'mon. We better get back. I bet Abe wants some breakfast of his own."

"Abe?"

"My dog. Abraham Lincoln, to be exact. Great president. Man of prayer." She winked at Sam. "I always name my pets after my heroes. And Abe is a good companion. If you stay around here a while and need a friend, Abe's great at listening to you talk out your frustration. Or sometimes he's good just to sit there and let you cry on his furry shoulder."

"Okay."

They walked about a mile to a small brick building that had Structure Street Youth Center painted on the windows in bright green letters. Inside it smelled like cinnamon apples. He glanced around and noticed a Ping-Pong table, an air hockey table, and a large TV with some couches.

Maggie took the leash off her big dog. "Let me go feed Abe and get my keys. There are some sodas in the fridge in the side room." Then Maggie hurried through a back door to an area that Sam assumed was where she lived. She left the door between the two areas open, and Sam could see a small living room and kitchen combo through the door.

Sam glanced around the large youth center and noticed that what looked like graffiti on the walls was actually names: Alexander, Tiffany, Megan, Mason. As he walked closer, Sam noticed that under each name was a single "I can" sentence.

I can stop lying.
I can graduate.
I can change.
I can—

The names and phrases went on around the room. Sam

walked around and looked at them, and read all the statements. A few were funny like, "I can learn to cross my eyes," but most were serious. As he walked, Abe came trotting into the room. Sam turned and kneeled.

"Hey, boy, how do you like it around here? I bet there are a lot of kids that come around here. If you could talk, I bet you could tell me all types of stories."

Sam sank onto the floor, sitting. He leaned his back against the cold, brick wall. "I don't even know what I'd write. I can—" Sam's mind thought about skateboarding and soccer and even football and his car. None of them seemed that important. He thought about his grandparents and about his brother and sister and even his dad, but it seemed that he was always *reacting* to them—not figuring out what he wanted. For a while he thought he wanted to be with his dad, but now he wasn't so sure. In fact, it was hard to know what he wanted, much less how to get it.

Sam sat for a while with Abe, just stroking him and petting the soft fur around his nose. And he continued to look at the words on the wall.

"I can—start to dream of the future," Sam finally mumbled. Saying those words caused his shoulders to quiver. He'd spent the last ten months mostly looking back. It hurt to think about moving forward. It almost felt as if being happy would mean he didn't miss his mom.

Yet, what would happen if he did dream? If he maybe considered graduation and what he would do afterward? Contemplate where he'd live? Talked about it with people instead of just coming up with his own plans and doing his own thing?

Maybe he would stay with his dad. Maybe not. Maybe he'd return to Nebraska and figure out what was next.

Sam's legs started to fall asleep, and he rose to shake them out. He turned as Maggie hurried into the room.

"Found my car keys," she called out in a singsong voice. "You ready?" She headed toward the front door.

"Actually, Maggie, um, I was wondering if I could use your phone. There's someone I need to call."

Chapter
Twenty-Four

Emily tried to hold in the chuckle as she watched her Uncle Pete making pancakes. When she'd come down from the shower he'd been staring at the page in the cookbook with intensity, and it wasn't until she saw what he was looking at that Emily even realized cookbooks told people how to make pancakes. She knew how to make them because she'd helped Grandma before. And from the looks of Uncle Pete's batter, she knew he'd done something wrong.

"Hey, Uncle Pete. Need help there?" Emily sidled up to him, staring at the thin, oily liquid in his bowl.

"Sure, kiddo. Why don't you set the table. I'm going to get these pancakes going."

"Uh, Uncle Pete . . ." She stared at the batter.

"Yeah?" He looked at her and raised his eyebrows. "Is there a problem?"

"Oh, no." Emily didn't want to make him feel bad. "I was just wondering if you'd like me to make some orange juice to go with the pancakes?"

"Sure, Emily. That will be great."

Christopher jogged down the stairs just as Uncle Pete had the first few pancakes made. Emily watched as Christopher approached his uncle with wide eyes.

"Uh, Uncle Pete. Those don't look right."

Uncle Pete puffed out his chest. "Well, they don't look the way Grandma makes them, but I'm sure they taste great!"

Christopher tore off a piece from one of the cooked pancakes, testing it.

"Mmm. Actually they sort of taste like donuts."

"Really?" Emily approached the kitchen counter and took a bite. They did taste sort of oily, but sweet too, like a donut. "Yeah, Uncle Pete. Maybe we don't even need to use syrup with these."

The knock at the door surprised Emily. She turned to see Uncle Bill standing there. He opened the door without waiting for them to answer and hurried inside.

Uncle Pete glanced over his shoulder. "Honestly, Bill. You really don't have to knock."

"Well, I don't want to overstep my bounds. Mom and Dad made that clear the other day."

Uncle Pete sighed, and he went back to flipping the pancakes, but he didn't say anything.

Uncle Bill glanced around the kitchen. His eyes darted between the sinkload of dishes and Christopher, who was still in his pajamas.

"Sort of running a little late this morning, aren't ya? Looks like the kids are gonna miss the bus."

"Oh." Uncle Pete glanced at the clock. "I—"

"Uncle Pete is going to drive us today," Emily interrupted. "Considering all that's going on with Sam, he thought it would be a good idea." Emily met Uncle Pete's gaze, nodding her head and encouraging him to go along with the story.

"Yeah, he's gonna drive us," Christopher took another bite of the pancake he'd tested earlier.

"Is that breakfast?" Uncle Bill approached the counter and glanced down at the thin, crisp pancakes.

"They're donut pancakes," Christopher offered. "A special recipe."

"Sure. If you say so." Uncle Bill tucked in his shirt, and his round paunch reminded Emily of her grandpa's gut, only not quite as big.

Uncle Pete smiled at Christopher and then at Emily, straightening his shoulders as he went back to making pancakes. It made Emily want to stick up for her youngest uncle more often.

"So, what are you doing out so early? Don't you have meetings and stuff?" Pete finished making the last pancake and turned off the griddle.

"Anna just thought it would be nice for me to pop in. You know what a worrywart she is."

"You really don't need to check in on us, Uncle Bill." Emily took the syrup out of the refrigerator. "But, since you're here, maybe *you* can give us a ride when you head back to work. That will leave time for Uncle Pete to straighten up the house before heading out to finish the morning chores."

She tossed her hair over her shoulder. "But, of course,

we don't want to send you to work hungry. Want some breakfast?"

Both her uncles looked at Emily with surprise. She smiled to herself as she sat down at the table.

"Just like her grandma," Uncle Bill muttered, making his way to the table and pulling out a chair. "If I could guess the future, I'd say Emily's another Charlotte in the making—bossing everyone around in such a kind way that you don't realize you've been bossed—"

The phone rang, interrupting Bill's words.

"I'll get it!" Emily leapt from her chair and hurried to the phone. "Maybe it's Grandma!"

Emily lifted the receiver to her ear. "Hello?"

"Hey, Ems." It was Sam's voice.

Emily sucked in a breath. "Sam!"

She turned to look at her uncles, and both stood and hurried to her.

"Do you need me to talk to him?" Uncle Bill held out his hand.

Emily shook her head. "Sam, where in the world are you? Do you know you got everyone scared out of their minds?" She couldn't stop the words that spilled out.

"Emily, let me talk." Uncle Pete also reached for the phone."

Emily held up her hand.

"I know. Is, uh, Grandma there?"

"No. Grandma is not here. She and Grandpa are on their way to Golden, Colorado, looking for you!"

"What? Are you serious? How did they know?"

"You're not the only one who knows how to figure things

out on the computer." Then Emily remembered the reason for Sam's trip. "So . . ." She lowered her voice. "Did you find Dad?"

She turned her back so she didn't have to see her uncles' faces.

"I want to say hello to Sam!" Christopher tugged on her arm, but Emily ignored him.

"Not yet," Sam answered. "I'm on my way over there right now. So . . . are Grandma and Grandpa here? Are they in Golden?"

"Not yet. They had to stay the night at a hotel somewhere because of the weather. But I think they're pretty close."

"Are they mad?" Sam's voice sounded anxious.

"Not really mad. They're more worried. What made you think—"

Emily felt the phone being tugged away and she turned to find Uncle Pete taking it.

"Hey, Sam, this is Uncle Pete. Where are you? Yes, I know you're in Golden. Where exactly? Who? Okay, that's cool someone there is helping you." Emily focused on the one-sided conversation. "Yeah, ask for the number."

Uncle Pete stretched the cord and found an envelope and a pen to write with.

"Who's helping him?" Uncle Bill followed Pete.

"Some woman at a youth center."

"A stranger? Sam's with a stranger?" Uncle Bill's eyebrows folded into a frown.

"Okay, go ahead." Uncle Pete wrote down an address. "Got it. I'm gonna give you a number too. It's Hannah's cell phone. Grandma is using it. Call her—" Uncle Pete paused.

"Uh-huh. Oh, and Sam, maybe you should wait to go see your dad. Ask Grandma and Grandpa to go with you. No, I think it will be okay. In fact I think they'd like to be there."

Emily leaned against the kitchen counter and began biting her fingernails. She'd just painted them yesterday but that didn't matter.

This is real. Sam is going to find our dad soon. After today things can be totally changed.

She glanced up, and her gaze met Uncle Bill's. He had the smallest smile on his face as he watched Uncle Pete. A look of approval.

Yep, I have a feeling today is a good beginning for change.

Chapter Twenty-Five

Sam glanced at the clock for the hundredth time. It had been almost two hours since he had called them, and his grandparents had yet to show up. His grandma had actually started crying on the phone. And like Uncle Pete said, they seemed happy to be able to go with Sam to find his dad. Mostly they seemed relieved that he was okay.

The youth room was quiet except for the television that was playing the first Indiana Jones movie. Neither he nor Maggie was really watching it.

Sam sat in the smaller loveseat with Abe curled up on his feet. The more time passed the more worried Sam became. The roads were bad. His grandpa's health wasn't that great. What if something had happened to him? Sam couldn't deal with that, knowing they had been coming after him.

He walked to the window and looked outside. Big flakes fell on the road. The beeping of some large machine neared, and Sam realized it was a snowplow. He just hoped that people were keeping the road clear for travelers.

"Did you try their cell phone?" he asked Maggie.

"Yes, still busy."

"You gave my grandparents easy directions to get here, didn't you?"

"Of course. You've already asked me twice." Maggie rose from the recliner and stood by him at the window.

"Maggie," Sam yawned wide. "Do you think my grandparents are going to be mad at me?"

"Well, Sam, you know them better than I do. What do you think?"

"I think they will—but they are probably more worried than anything."

"I bet you're right."

"Do you think they're going to let me see my dad? Or were they just saying that?"

"Well, from everything you've told me, they seem like honest folks."

"Yeah, and they believe in keeping their word too."

Just then Sam noticed a familiar truck parking outside the center. Then his grandma climbed from the truck.

He felt like running out and wrapping his arms around her neck, but held back.

He hesitantly walked to the door and opened it.

"Sam!" his grandmother exclaimed, rushing toward him with open arms.

"Hi, Grandma. I—I'm sorry—for everything." Sam couldn't hold himself back any longer. He wrapped his arms around her shoulders and squeezed hard. "I'm glad you made it okay."

His grandma pulled back, and he watched as she wiped tears from her face.

His grandfather followed. "Sam." It was all he said, and then he put his hand on Sam's shoulder. Sam couldn't read his emotions from his face. "So, I hear you've found Kevin Slater?"

"Yes, I can go there, right? Today?"

His grandma nodded. "Yes, but, well, Grandpa wants to talk about things first. To let you know how much we'd like you to stay with us, even if you do find your dad."

Sam scratched the top of his head. "I thought you'd want to kick me out after this."

"We are a little frustrated with the problems you've caused, but you can never do anything that will make us want to give up on you."

Sam glanced at the wall behind them and remembered his thoughts from earlier that day. "Yeah, I think a plan is good."

"Can we use the bathroom first to freshen up?"

Sam introduced them to Maggie, and she led them toward the bathrooms.

Sam scratched Abe's ear. "Man, you have it easy being a dog. No family to deal with, just lots of walks and pats." Sam curled back on the couch and used the remote to click off the television.

Then again, Sam realized, families were work, but they were worth it. To be cared for was something he'd taken for granted.

As he thought about what the next hour would bring, he realized that whatever the outcome, he'd always have some place to fall back to. Some place to go. Realizing that made him think of something else he could write on the wall:

Sam.

I can go home.

Charlotte attempted to eat the nice lunch that Maggie had made for them—grilled-cheese sandwiches, sliced cucumber, and boiled eggs. Instead, she hardly could swallow a bite. She was worried about Bob, who had dark circles under his eyes. And she was frustrated with Sam, who acted as if today was the most exciting day of his life. In fact, he could hardly sit still as he ate, rising to check the weather outside, folding and refolding the slip of paper in his hand that had Kevin Slater's address on it, petting the dog and whispering in its ear as if they had a secret of their own.

Mostly, Charlotte was worried about coming face to face with Kevin Slater again. She was angry with the man for abandoning his family ten years ago. And although over the years she'd thought about him and prayed for him, she'd never expected there would come a day when she'd have to see him, speak to him. It made all the pain real, fresh.

As the minutes ticked by, Charlotte could tell that Bob wanted to talk to Sam. Maggie must have realized it too. "I'm going to take Abe for a quick walk around the block. When I get back I'll draw you a small map to lead you to that address you're looking for."

Abe seemed almost reluctant to leave Sam, and Maggie had to use a dog treat to lead the lab out the door. When she left, Sam leaned back in his chair and folded his arms as if he was preparing himself for the lecture to come. And it did.

"Sam, do you know how much you worried your grandmother and me?" Bob leaned forward in his chair and rested his arms on the table. "You lied to us. You stole from your grandmother. You put your life at risk."

"Yes, I know. I—I'm sorry." Sam turned to Charlotte and she could see sincerity in his gaze.

"You should have come to us," Bob continued. "We would have made a plan. We would have come with you."

"Honestly?" Sam asked, pulling his hoodie over his head. "I thought you would have tried to talk me out of it."

"Maybe we would have. But we've always wanted what's best for you, Sam." Charlotte reached over and patted his hand. "We're stubborn in our old age, but not heartless. We realize how hard all this has been on you.

"But I just want you to know that no matter what happens today, you're welcome back on the farm. Of course, you'll be doing extra chores to make up for all the expenses, but you'll always have a place with us."

"All right." Sam nodded slowly. "Yeah, that makes sense. Thanks for, uh, going with me." Then he stood and moved to the door where his sneakers were. He put them on and glanced back with a wince. "Now, can we just get this over with? I can't handle the anxiety anymore."

Charlotte glanced at the lunch dishes and thought about insisting they help Maggie clean up before they left. But deep inside she felt the same way. She wanted it done. Over.

"We can do the dishes when we get back." She rose and slid on her jacket. "I'm with Sam, Bob. Let's get this over with. And once we see Kevin we can discuss where to go from there."

Maggie got back from her walk and gave them directions. It was only a fifteen-minute drive before they were turning down a street lined with apartment complexes. The buildings had peeling paint and looked foreboding against the gray sky. Charlotte looked at the numbers and then glanced at the directions Maggie had given her. "There it is, the first building on the right."

Bob parked the truck in the visitor's parking section, and Charlotte turned to Sam, who was wedged between her and Bob on the front seat.

"Would you like us to walk up there with you?" she asked.

"Actually, I feel as if it's something I need to do myself. I'll come back and get you in a few minutes—depending on what my dad says."

"Okay," Charlotte opened the door and slid from the seat. "We'll be waiting."

Then she climbed back in and watched as Sam reached the concrete steps that led to the second story. He took them slowly as if his body was too heavy to carry him upward. As she watched him, Charlotte's heart felt heavy too.

So much, Lord, for a young man to handle. Be with him. Help him. No matter what happens, give Sam the peace to know this is how things were meant to turn out . . .

And, Lord, give me the same peace. No matter what comes of this moment.

Chapter
Twenty-Six

Standing outside the door, Sam could hear the sound of the television playing inside. It sounded like cartoons—Scooby Doo. His stomach flipped as he realized that cartoon had been his dad's favorite.

He wanted to glance back at his grandparents, to see if they were watching, but then changed his mind because he knew they were. The air was cold and nipped at his nose. Sam breathed in a long breath and then let it out slowly. Then, gathering up enough nerve, he raised his fist and knocked hard.

Two seconds later the door opened. He'd been expecting his father's face, but instead he saw a young boy with blond hair standing there.

"Yeah?" the boy asked.

"Trevor, who is it?" a woman's voice called.

"I don't know." He shouted back. "Who're you?"

Sam opened his mouth and then closed it again, wondering if this kid was his brother. He sort of looked like Christopher, but not really. Sam's stomach rumbled, and he was sure he was going to throw up. He'd never considered the fact that his father might have a new family—a different wife. Different kids.

"I'm sorry, can I help you?" A thin woman wearing a large Broncos sweatshirt approached the door. Her hair was short and dark. She looked nice enough. "If you're selling something I'm afraid I can't help you out." She started to shut the door.

"No." Sam found his voice. "I'm not selling anything. I'm looking for someone. Kevin Slater."

The woman paused, and her brow furrowed. "What do you want with Kevin?"

"To talk with him, that's all." Sam took a step back, hoping to show the woman he meant no harm.

The woman patted the boy's head. "Trevor, you can go back and watch cartoons now." The boy did as he was directed and the woman stepped closer to Sam.

"I'm sorry. You're too late. Kevin hasn't lived here for three months, at least. If he owes you money, then don't come to me. I don't have anything to do with that."

Sam felt himself sink into a dark cloud of disappointment. "Do you have any idea where he went?"

She shrugged. "Sorry, can't tell you that. All I know is we got into a big fight and he took off. He didn't come back. Didn't call. You'd think he'd treat me more decent than that after as long as we'd been together. You aren't in trouble with the law, are you?"

"No. I, uh—" Sam swallowed hard as he prepared to ask the next question, realizing that the kid was most likely his half brother.

"And, uh, how long was that? How long were you together?"

The woman eyed him again, studying his face. "Nosy, aren't you? But I guess it doesn't matter now. Almost a year.

Just when my kid got used to having him around he's gone. Just like they all do." The woman's shoulders sank.

"And you're sure you don't know where he went?"

The woman shook her head and began to close the door. "No, like I said before—"

"Okay, we'll, uh, thanks," Sam said, turning. *Three months?* His dad could be anywhere. On the other side of town or halfway around the world. He thought about everything he'd done and all those he'd hurt in the process. And for what? For nothing. Absolutely nothing.

Sam moved down the first two steps, and then he felt a hand on his shoulder.

"Hey, young man, wait."

Sam turned.

The woman stood there on the landing in slippers and studied his face again.

"Are you Sam?"

Sam's hand gripped the rail. "Yes. How did you know?"

"From your pictures. Come inside and we can talk. It's too cold out here to go into everything." It was Sam now who eyed the woman suspiciously.

"Come on now, I don't bite. I assume you came a long way. From San Diego?"

"No, I, well I don't live in San Diego anymore. And my grandparents. They are waiting for me in the car."

"Okay, yeah," the woman stepped inside the house. "They can come in too. The house is a mess, but I have some things to show you. Things you'll want to see."

"I'll go get them." Sam hurried down the steps again, the weight he'd been carrying around for the past few weeks lifted. His dad wasn't here, and this woman didn't know where he was. But the fact that he'd talked about Sam— that he'd showed this woman photos. Well, that meant something, didn't it?

Sam jogged to his grandpa's truck, being careful not to slip on the ice. His grandma opened the door as she watched him approach.

"My dad isn't here, but his old, uh, girlfriend wants to talk to us. She says she has some things for me."

"Does she know where he is?" Grandpa asked.

"No, he's been gone for three months."

Sam looked at his grandma, sure he saw relief on her face.

"Okay," she said. "We're here. We might as well talk to this woman."

Sam led the way through the snowy sidewalk and up the stairs. His father had left, but had not forgotten him. It was something to cling to, no matter how small it was.

Chapter Twenty-Seven

Charlotte glanced around the small apartment, noting the young boy sitting in front of the television set. The apartment was sparsely furnished. The woman invited them to sit around the dining room table.

"I'm Marla, by the way."

"Nice to meet you. I'm Charlotte, and this is my husband, Bob. And, of course, you've met our grandson, Sam."

The woman sat across from Charlotte, her hands clasped together. "Wow, I wasn't expecting company today. I'm afraid I don't have any snacks to offer you."

"No, that's not necessary. We've just had lunch, and we're getting on the road soon and heading back to Nebraska." Charlotte glanced at Sam, wondering if that was his plan. They hadn't talked about him returning home with them, but she hoped that he would.

"I'm sorry I can't be of more help. I have no idea where Kevin is. We got in a fight, you see, and he left. He always came back before, but not this time. He left most of his things, including the items I was going to show Sam."

"How long ago did he leave?" Bob asked. Charlotte knew her husband honestly didn't care if they ever found Kevin

Slater, but perhaps he was trying to show Sam that he was concerned and did want to help.

"Three months ago. Right before Thanksgiving."

The young boy ran into the room. "Mommy, I'm thirsty."

"Just a minute. Can't you see I'm talking?"

"I can get him something." Charlotte rose.

"Sure, thanks. The glasses are in the first cupboard on the right. There is juice in the fridge."

Charlotte opened the cupboard and found a faded plastic Superman cup. In the refrigerator she saw a loaf of bread, a half-carton of juice, and little else.

She poured juice for the boy and handed it to him with a smile. "Here you go. What's your name?"

"Trevor."

Charlotte extended her hand. "Nice to meet you, Trevor. I'm Grandma Charlotte." She closed the refrigerator door and noticed a drawing.

"Did you draw this?" Charlotte asked. In the dining room she could hear Marla talking to Bob and Sam about Kevin Slater, saying how they met working at a mini-mart together, and they dated for six months before moving in together.

Trevor smiled, and he pulled the picture off the fridge. "That's me and my mom and Daddy Kevin, but he left and my mom cried a lot."

Another family left in heartbreak.

"I'm sorry to hear that, Trevor." She kneeled before him. "Make sure and give your mommy lots of hugs, okay? I think it will help you both feel better."

Trevor nodded, and Charlotte returned to the dining room table.

"Trevor had gotten attached to Kevin. I had too. I thought for sure he'd come back, especially for the things he left." Marla rose. "Hold on. Let me show you."

Marla held a small shoe box. She set it before Sam.

"Uh, thanks." Sam looked at Bob and then at Charlotte.

"Go ahead. Let's see it." Bob tapped the top of the box.

Sam opened it, his fingers leaving imprints in the dust on the lid.

"Mr. Cuddl—" Sam's voice caught in his throat. He covered his face with his large hand, and then shrugged his shoulders as if trying to shrug off the emotion. "It's my bear. I had it as a kid. I thought it was lost."

"There's more. Underneath." Marla scooted her chair closer to Sam as she peered inside.

Sam took out a small pile of papers. "Ticket stubs from a Padres game. A photo of me and Emily. And look, the newspaper clipping from Christopher's birth announcement." Sam held something else up and then paused. The color drained from his face.

"Sam, are you okay?" Charlotte reached across the table and touched his arm.

"It's a photo of Mom." Sam placed it on the table, and Charlotte felt the tears coming before she could stop them.

"Look, her hair was still long. She cut it after you were born. I can't tell from the way she's standing, but I'd guess this was taken when she was pregnant with you. See—" Charlotte pointed to the waves cresting behind Denise. "It's at the ocean. It must have been right after they arrived in California."

Marla tried to force a smile, and Charlotte realized it

must be awkward for her to hear them talking this way about Kevin Slater's ex-wife.

"And where is your mom now?" Marla asked. "Is she still living in California?"

Sam lowered his head. "No. She—"

"She passed away last year. Sam's living with us now, in Nebraska." Charlotte wiped away a lone tear that pooled in the corner of her eye.

"Oh, I see. I'm so sorry. I didn't know." Marla paused and turned to Sam. "And your dad didn't know. He would have told me, I'm sure, if he did."

Sam shrugged. "It doesn't matter now. Things are good." He looked across the table to Charlotte. Then he looked at Bob. "My brother and sister and I, we're doing okay. The whole thing has taken some getting used to, but Nebraska's home." His eyes met Charlotte's. "It's as good as it can be without my mom, I suppose."

Charlotte felt warmth filling her chest. They had their grandson back, and though he'd still have consequences to face for his actions, she knew everything would be all right. He'd called Nebraska home—which is more than she'd hoped for. She smiled at her grandson as she rose. "We should be heading out."

"I'm ready." Sam stood and tucked the box under his arm. "I'm ready to get home."

About the Author

Tricia Goyer is the author of eight novels, six nonfiction books, and one children's book. She was named Mount Hermon Christian Writers Conference Writer of the Year in 2003. In 2005, her book *Life Interrupted* was a finalist for the Gold Medallion and her novel *Night Song* won American Christian Fiction Writers Book of the Year for Long Historical Romance. In 2006, her novel *Dawn of a Thousand Nights* also won Book of the Year for Long Historical. Tricia has written more than three hundred articles for national publications and hundreds of Bible study notes for the *Women of Faith Study Bible*. Tricia lives with her husband and three kids in Montana, where she homeschools, leads children's church, and mentors teenage mothers.

A Note from the Editors

This original book was created by the Books and Inspirational Media Division of Guideposts, the world's leading inspirational publisher. Founded in 1945 by Dr. Norman Vincent Peale and Ruth Stafford Peale, Guideposts helps people from all walks of life achieve their maximum personal and spiritual potential. Guideposts is committed to communicating positive, faith-filled principles for people everywhere to use in successful daily living.

Our publications include award-winning magazines such as *Guideposts* and *Angels on Earth*, best-selling books, and outreach services that demonstrate what can happen when faith and positive thinking are applied in day-to-day life.

For more information, visit us at www.guideposts.com, call (800) 431-2344 or write Guideposts, PO Box 5815, Harlan, Iowa 51593.